BRODIE

Texas Rascals Book 8

LORI WILDE

S he couldn't go through with it.

Deannie Hollis sat on the antique four-poster bed in the south bedroom of the rambling Texas ranch house that until fifteen years ago had belonged to the Hollis family for four generations. Her parents had conceived her in this very bedroom.

Now all she had to do to reclaim her birthright was to walk down the aisle and say "I do" to Brodie True-blood. It was that simple, and that complicated.

Tears slipped down her cheeks and pooled on the white lace collar of her western-cut wedding gown. A bouquet of white roses and baby's breath rested in her trembling hands, and a salty lump burned her throat.

Twisting Brodie's engagement ring on her finger, Deannie shook her head, trying her best to fight the guilt clutching her heart. Her pearl cluster earrings danced below her earlobes, and the mesh bridal veil brushed lightly against her shoulders.

She could not do this. Brodie deserved so much better. Sniffling, she reached for a tissue.

A knock sounded at the door.

"C-c-come in." Deannie hiccupped and smoothed her white satin skirt with one hand.

Her sister-in-law to be, Emma Trueblood, poked her head in the door. "Preacher's here. Everyone's waiting."

"Could you give me ten more minutes?"

"Cold feet?" Emma swished into the room in a lavender whirl and shut the door behind her. She plopped down on the bed beside Deannie.

"Sort of."

"Oh, honey, you know you're getting the best man in Presidio County."

"I know." *That* was the problem.

Emma patted her hand. "It'll be all right, I promise. If you love Brodie, and he loves you, nothing else matters."

But Emma was wrong.

Dead wrong.

Because Deannie had a dark secret.

"I know my marriage to Kenny isn't perfect," Emma chattered, "but we're working things out. And believe it or not, after seven years, our life together is better than ever."

Deannie knew. She'd seen Kenny's transformation firsthand. "I'm glad you guys are happy. You deserve all the happiness in the world."

"We owe it to you and Brodie. If it weren't for you two, Kenny and I would still be separated."

"Naw, Kenny's a good man. He would have come to his senses eventually."

Emma hugged Deannie. "Come on, woman, don't let marriage scare you. It really *is* worth the effort."

Marriage didn't scare her, deceiving Brodie True-blood did.

"I need five more minutes alone," Deannie pleaded. "Please, Emma."

"Okay." Looking puzzled, her matron-of-honor left the room.

Deannie tried to take a deep breath, but anxiety twisted around her throat, and claustrophobia gripped her stomach.

She had to get out of here.

Leave.

Flee.

Run.

Now.

Today.

This minute.

Before it was too late.

Springing to her feet, she dashed to the window and pushed back the curtain. Brodie's pickup sat around back, already desecrated by well-wishers. White shoe polish announcing *Just Married* muddied the windows, and dozens of aluminum cans dangled from the bumper. Even if she had access to the keys, they parked cars around the circular driveway, blocking her exit.

Stuck, stranded.

What to do?

She couldn't face Brodie, couldn't call off the wedding while looking him in the face. She was too big a coward for that. Couldn't bear to see the trust go out of his eyes.

Strains of the wedding march came from the living room as their neighbor, Bonnie McNally, played the piano.

In her mind, she saw the gaily decorated living room —vases of roses, white crepe paper streamers, satin doves, silk bows. She knew little Buster was there, clutching a pillow with their wedding rings pinned to it. And so was sweet Angel, dressed in ruffles and lace, carrying a basketful of white rose petals. Their friends, dressed in their best finery, gathered in the living room, waiting to witness the union of Brodie Trueblood and Deannie McCellan.

Only she wasn't Deannie McCellan as everyone believed.

Closing her eyes, she saw Brodie standing before the altar, his dark hair combed back off his forehead, his brown eyes shining with radiant love. A love that would die the instant he learned the truth about her.

Deannie moaned and fisted her hands as sorrow writhed through her. Better to leave him at the altar than marry him and live a lie.

She'd tried to convince herself that love was enough. Self-denial had led her this far, but her conscience balked at finishing her mission. She could not do it.

Peering out the window again, Deannie searched the grounds below, desperate for a solution. She spotted Brodie's horse, Ranger, saddled in the paddock.

Yes. That was it. She would take Ranger and clear out. Once she got to Rascal, she'd figure out where to go from there.

Decision made, Deannie moved aside the sash and raised the window. With both hands, she pushed out the screen. Hiking her dress around her waist, she placed a booted foot on the sill. One look at those white boots and her heart lurched in her throat.

Just two weeks ago, she and Brodie had gone to El Paso, where he'd picked out the boots especially for their wedding, saying they were perfect for his cowgirl bride.

Don't think about it. Just go.

She hesitated a moment, calculating the distance to the ground from the second story. Taking a deep breath, she gathered her skirt in her hands.

"Here goes," she whispered and jumped.

Deannie landed feet first and stumbled backward from the impact. Recovering, she ran across the yard toward the paddock, flung open the gate, and clicked her tongue at Ranger.

Obediently, the horse came to her. Pulse thudding, Deannie swung into the saddle.

The cool September breeze ruffled her hair as she grabbed the reins and aimed Ranger west toward the setting sun. Clouds bunched on the horizon, threatening rain.

Any minute now Brodie would discover her gone. Any minute the atmosphere would change from festive to gloomy. Any minute Brodie's heart would break, shattered just as surely as her own, their hopes and dreams crushed like rose petals in a hailstorm.

Oh, why had she fallen in love with him?

Regret, heavy and unshakable, filled her. Blinking back more tears, Deannie galloped across the prairie. Her veil streaming out behind her, her train whipping against the saddle. Her hands, encased in soft white gloves, clutched the reins in a death grip.

Her mind jettisoned back to that fateful day four months ago. The day she returned to Rascal, hell-bent on revenge.

2

F *our months earlier*

"I'M LOOKING FOR RAFE TRUEBLOOD," DEANNIE Hollis said to the man behind the bar.

She swept her gaze through the dimly lit honky-tonk. Even at four o'clock on a Monday afternoon, Lonesome Dove was crowded. A sad commentary on the rough economic times in Presidio County. Too many people out of work. Too many people spending their unemployment checks drowning their sorrows. Too many people looking for love in all the wrong places.

"Well, sugar, I'm afraid you're about two weeks too late," the bartender drawled, leaning on the counter with both elbows.

"What do you mean?" Deannie asked, raising her

voice above the jukebox where Hank Williams, Jr. sang about family traditions. "Rafe Trueblood's dead."

Deannie stared at the bartender in stunned disbelief. It couldn't be true.

Rafe dead? No! Not after she'd spent the past fifteen years plotting her revenge against the man who'd cheated her father out of his house, his hometown, and her inheritance.

She'd counted the years, months, weeks, days, hours until she was old enough, wily enough, and accomplished enough at poker to challenge that thieving Rafe Trueblood to a card game and win back the family ranch the same way her daddy had lost it.

"Yep. Keeled right over during a poker game. I, for one, will sorely miss the man. Rafe spent a good three hundred dollars a week in here. He was a big tipper, too."

Deannie sucked in her breath. Her whole body trembled. The smell of stale cigarettes hung in the air, choking her.

The noise from the jukebox echoed in her ears. A dry, bitter taste glutted her mouth. Blinking, she clutched the bar with both hands.

"Sugar?" The bartender's burly face blurred before her. "Are you all right?"

Her mouth opened, but no words came out.

The bartender hurried around the bar and gently pushed her down onto a stool. "Rafe a good friend of yours, was he?"

"I didn't expect this." She lifted a hand to her throat.

"Well, fifty-five years of hard, fast living finally caught up with him."

Staring at the scarred linoleum floor, Deannie tried to come to grips with the news. What was she going to do now? Her life's goal of reclaiming the family homestead had died along with the gambler.

"Rafe's son, Kenny, is in the back room," the bartender said, squatting down in front of her. "I don't normally let strangers go back there because sometimes the boys indulge in a little illegal gambling, but seein' as how you were a friend of Rafe's..."

"Thank you," Deannie whispered. She'd forgotten Rafe Trueblood had two sons. She'd only been seven when she and her daddy were forced from their home at Willow Creek Ranch and moved into a squalid one-bedroom apartment in Midland.

From what the bartender said, Kenny Trueblood must have followed in his father's disreputable footsteps. Pressing a palm to her forehead, Deannie considered her next move. Should she give up and go back... where? She had no home. The only real home she'd ever had was right here in Rascal.

Why did she have to change her plans? She could win Willow Creek Ranch back from Kenny just as easily as she could have won it from Rafe.

Maybe even easier.

"This way." The bartender took her by the hand and led her past a string of curious customers eyeing them from the bar.

They pushed through two sets of double doors and into a storeroom dominated with fat-bellied men and a poker table. Six pairs of suspicious eyes swung to take in Deannie.

"Kenny," the bartender said, gesturing to the youngest, most attractive man in the room. "This little gal came in looking for your daddy."

A huge smile rippled across Kenny Trueblood's face as his gaze raked the length of Deannie's body. His stark once-over left her feeling unclothed. Crossing her arms over her chest, she met his stare with a frown.

"You're a little young," Kenny assessed, "even for the old man's eclectic tastes."

"I wasn't his girlfriend," Deannie replied.

The man's intense scrutiny didn't buffalo her. This wasn't the first time she'd gotten ogled. She'd spent her fair share of time in honky-tonks following after her father, and she could take care of herself.

"I gotta get back to work." The bartender jerked his thumb toward the bar. "You fellas play nice."

"We're always nice," one man grumbled and swallowed a long swig from his beer. The rest of them chuckled.

Deannie lifted her chin and tried her best to look tough. This was it. The moment she'd been waiting for, although the showdown was anticlimactic after the news of Rafe's death.

"Why did you come looking for my old man?" Kenny asked, dusting off an empty chair and patting the seat. Tentatively, Deannie inched over and perched next to Kenny. He smelled of beer and peanuts and aftershave.

"I came to play cards," she declared. "I heard if you

want to test your skills at Texas Hold 'Em, Rafe True-blood is the man to beat."

One fellow hooted. "Are you serious?"

The guy sitting on Deannie's right choked on his beer and sputtered. His friend pounded him on the back.

"What's this?" The bearded giant shuffling cards raised an eyebrow. "The kid thinks she could have beaten Rafe?"

Kenny held up a hand and tried hard to disguise his smile. "Come on, Lou, give the lady a chance. If she can pay, let her play."

"Are you saying we should deal her in?" Lou looked incredulous.

"Got something against taking money from children?" Kenny asked.

"I'm no child," Deannie insisted, thrusting out her jaw. "I'm twenty-two."

"Hmm, you look younger," Kenny said.

"All right." Lou dealt the cards. "If you're dumb enough to play, ante up, girly. It's a ten-dollar minimum."

Deannie pushed a lock of hair from her forehead. "I'll need some chips."

"Here you go, sugar," one man said, presenting her with a rack of poker chips.

"Don't," she growled, "call me sugar."

"Yes, ma'am." The man grinned. "Feisty. You'll fit right in."

As if she wanted to fit in with this bunch.

"What's your name?" Kenny asked, leaning closer

and striking a match against his thumbnail to light a cigar.

The action, so much like his father's, sent a shudder through her at the memory. "Deannie McCellan," she said, using her mother's maiden name.

"Where are you from, Deannie?"

"Midland."

"Where'd you hear about Rafe?"

Deannie shrugged. "Here and there."

"You can do better than that." Kenny casually draped one arm across the back of her

chair.

Deannie stared hard at him until Kenny laughed nervously and removed it.

"Keep that up..." chortled the man who'd called her sugar. "...and you'll pull back a stump."

"My father used to play cards with a man named Gil Hollis. From what I understand, Rafe was such a good card player he won Mr. Hollis's ranch in a poker game. Is that correct?" She reeled out the lie she'd practiced smooth as a velvet ribbon.

Looking uncomfortable, Kenny gnawed on the end of his cigar. "Yeah. It's true."

"Your father must have been some gambler, Mr. Trueblood. Did you know Gil Hollis got so depressed he committed suicide over the shame of losing his family homestead? He never recovered from the humiliation." A hard bite of hatred crept into her voice; she heard it but prayed the men didn't.

Kenny cleared his throat and dropped his gaze. "No. I wasn't aware of that. Sorry to hear about it. But a bet's a bet. It wasn't Rafe's fault that Hollis was a weak fool."

Deannie bit down hard on her bottom lip to contain the jabbing burst of anger shooting through her at Kenny's callousness. The man was speaking about her daddy! How she longed to tell him exactly what she thought about him and all the scum-of-the-earth Truebloods.

"Are we gonna play cards, or we gonna chat like the ladies at Dorothy's Curl Up and Dye?" Lou grunted.

Just then the door creaked open.

Raising her head, Deannie looked up to see a tall, lean cowboy silhouetted in the light from the bar.

He walked with an easy, self-confident stride. His mouth was set in a hard, firm line, his brown-eyed gaze glancing harshly around the table. Settling his hands on his low-slung hips, he stared at Deannie, then shifted his attention to Kenny and back again.

The look flitting across his face told Deannie he'd made an erroneous assumption about her relationship with Kenny.

"Dammit, Kenny," the man exploded, his voice booming in the room's small confines. "What in the hell are you up to?"

"Don't get your underwear in a knot, little brother; it's not what you think."

"Hey, Brodie, pull up a chair," Lou invited.

"I got better things to do than get drunk and lose money at cards," Brodie said. "For your information, Kenny, while you're sitting here playing footsie with some underage bar dolly, your wife's in labor with your third child. Thought you might like to know."

This Trueblood was a sight to behold. He held his head high, his shoulders straight. He was a man of principle. Deannie read his character in his stance, and the way he chose his words.

Brodie's nostrils flared, and his bottom lip curled in disgust as he glowered at his brother.

Deannie's heart raced. He looked like tightly contained dynamite. He would not explode unprovoked, but heaven help the creature who earned this man's wrath.

Kenny stood, his chair scraping loudly across the cement floor. "Hey! Don't get high and mighty with me. You aren't married—you don't understand what it's like. Besides, Emma and I are separated. She's the one who left me, remember?"

"I wonder why." Brodie snorted, turned on his heels, and stalked out the door.

The room fell silent. Nobody looked at Kenny.

"Guess you'll be wantin' me to cash you out, huh?" Lou grunted.

"What the hell for?" Frowning, Kenny knocked back the rest of his beer.

"You're not going to the hospital?" Kenny's cavalier behavior shocked Deannie, but why? She shouldn't be surprised. He *was* Rafe Trueblood's son.

"Aww." Kenny waved a hand. "Emma labors for a good ten hours, and Brodie overreacts. I got lots of time. Ante up, everyone."

❧

SOMETIMES, BRODIE TRUEBLOOD WANTED TO TAKE HIS older brother by the front of the shirt and shake him silly. Unfortunately, Kenny had inherited their father's disreputable tendencies, drinking and gambling chief among them.

Now it seemed Kenny had added womanizing to the list.

Gritting his teeth, Brodie blasted from the parking lot. Who was the hot young redhead sitting next to Kenny? Brodie didn't recognize her, and he knew most everyone in Rascal.

That skimpy little outfit she'd been wearing spoke volumes. The emerald green color set off her fiery hair, and the silky material slid across her skin like rippling water. Though he'd tried not to notice, the deep, plunging V-neckline announced to the world she was proud of her cleavage and rightfully so.

He had to admit Kenny's good taste. The woman was a stunner. Even in the dim bar lighting, her well-sculpted features arrested him, from her high cheekbones to her slender, aristocratic nose. She was far classier than the typical barroom groupie.

Question was, what in the hell was she doing with Kenny? Finding out his brother had a third child on the way would probably put a crimp in her feelings for him.

Brodie turned his pickup truck toward Presidio County Hospital. Somebody ought to be there with Emma since his brother wasn't man enough to own up to his responsibilities. Sometimes the thankless chore of single-handedly redeeming the Trueblood name was an exhausting job.

Why did Kenny treat his wife so shabbily? Couldn't his brother see the pain he was causing the mother of his children? Shame for his brother's behavior burned

Brodie's craw. He hoped like hell Emma never found out about that redhead.

Again, Brodie wondered about the beautiful stranger. There was something provocative about her. The tilt of her head, maybe, or the gleam in her eyes. No matter. He knew the type—sexy as hell but interested in only one thing—money.

Yep. That redhead spelled trouble. Hadn't Rafe dallied with a long string of such women? They'd brought problems.

Brodie winced.

He hated remembering the bad things his father had done to his mother. Cheating on her, gambling away the grocery money, disappearing for days at a time, then turning up drunk as a skunk. Or else Mama would get a call from one jailhouse or the other, wanting her to come post the old man's bail.

The only thing worthwhile Rafe Trueblood had ever done was win Willow Creek Ranch and even that was an ill-gotten gain.

But despite the underhanded way his father had gotten the ranch, Brodie loved Willow Creek with all his heart. The place meant everything to him.

It was home.

Until Rafe cheated the ranch away from Gil Hollis, the Truebloods had lived a roller-coaster life. Moving from one shack to the next, flying high when Rafe hit it big in a poker game, subsisting on rice and beans for weeks when he lost money on the ponies.

Then one drunken night, Rafe had lucked out and buffaloed poor Gil Hollis into betting his entire inheritance on one hand of cards.

At last his mother had a home of her own. He and Kenny had finished high school in Rascal. For the first time in his life, they'd lived in one place long enough to make friends. Although it had been tough in the beginning. Not many of the townsfolk were happy to hear that one of their own had been swindled by an itinerant gambler like Rafe Trueblood.

Brodie had tried to justify his father. Losing the ranch was Gil Hollis' own fault, he'd rationalized. The man should never have gambled away something as precious as Willow Creek. Then he'd discovered that Gil Hollis had only started drinking and gambling after his wife's tragic death in a riding accident.

Braking for a stoplight at the corner of Ninth and Gardenia, Brodie remembered the day he'd gone to his father and asked him to give the ranch back to Mr. Hollis and his daughter. Dang if he could recall that little girl's name.

Rafe had laughed in his face and called him a "bleeding-heart pansy." Brodie frowned at the ugly memory. Dear old Dad. Quite the sentimentalist.

Unable to help Mr. Hollis, Brodie had done the next best thing. He'd vowed to make Willow Creek one of the most successful ranches in Presidio County. Over the years, no thanks to Rafe and Kenny, Brodie had achieved that goal.

Willow Creek now boasted over six hundred head of cattle and four hundred sheep. His hay crop was phenomenal, his business acumen legendary. Last year, when most farms and ranches struggled to break even, Willow Creek had cleared over one hundred thousand dollars in profit. Brodie Trueblood had done Gil Hollis proud.

Yes, he'd accomplished what he'd first set out to do at the naïve age of fourteen. He'd been interested in the operation from the very beginning, spending most of his spare time with the ranch foreman, Cooter Gates.

He learned about cattle and hay and what it meant to be a good rancher. By age eighteen, the year his mother died of cancer, Brodie was running the ranch, while Rafe and Kenny spent their time in honky-tonks and pool halls, living off the sweat of his brow.

The light turned green, and Brodie accelerated.

He'd thrown so much of himself into Willow Creek, he'd had no time for a personal life. Now, at twenty-nine, Brodie wondered what it would be like to have his own wife and kids. For the first time, he was jealous of Kenny. Jealous and angry at the way his older brother mistreated his family blessings.

Would he ever find his true love? A kind, tender-hearted woman like his mother. A woman who longed for a family and would cherish Willow Creek as much as he did.

Oddly enough, the image of that redheaded girl back at the bar flitted through his mind.

Don't be ridiculous. That gal might be up for a good time, but he needed to get tangled up with her like he needed a frontal lobotomy.

3

The stack of poker chips in front of Deannie kept growing.

Teasing derision had turned to grudging respect as she won hand after hand. For fifteen years, she'd sat in her tiny bedroom way into the wee hours of the night shuffling, dealing, learning the rules.

For fifteen years, she'd followed her father from bars to honky-tonks to the back-alley gambling parlors, and she'd absorbed everything like a sponge, thirsty for the key to her revenge. For fifteen years, she'd thought of only one thing—winning Willow Creek Ranch back from those worthless Truebloods.

Deannie Hollis had come here with a mission, but suddenly she discovered she was also having fun. It was worth every ounce of effort she'd put into perfecting her skills to watch the look on Kenny's face as he lost again and again.

Her only regret—that Rafe Trueblood wasn't the one sitting beside her.

"Where'd you learn to play poker like that?" Lou grumbled, drumming his hammy fingers on the table and frowning at her over his fan of cards.

"My daddy taught me."

"Who's your daddy? If he's from around here, I bet we know him."

"Er..." Deannie hesitated, scrambling to invent a fictitious name. "Joe McCellan."

Lou shook his head. "You ever heard of the guy, Kenny?"

"No, but I'm sure Rafe knew him. Where did you say you were from, Deannie?" Kenny angled her a glance.

"Midland. How many cards do you want?" Deannie asked, grateful for an excuse to change the subject. She was terrified they would catch her in a lie.

"I'm tapped out." One man threw down his cards in disgust.

"Me, too." Another player nodded.

"Too rich for my blood," added the man who'd called her sugar.

"I'll take four cards," Lou said.

Deannie swung her gaze to Kenny. Her pulse sped up. She didn't expect to win the ranch back in one game. She knew it would take time and probably a lot more liquor than was swirling in Kenny's bloodstream.

But she'd already taken him for seven hundred dollars. Not a bad start. "Well, Mr. Trueblood?"

Kenny laid his cards facedown on the table. "Thanks to your phenomenal card-playing abilities, I'm afraid I'm out of money, Miss McCellan."

Her bottom lip twitched. She couldn't let him get

away, not this easily. "You could always put something up for collateral."

"What's my Apple watch worth to you?" he asked, turning his wrist over. His eyes widened. "Glory, look at the time. I'd better get on to the hospital before Emma dominoes."

Deannie laid a hand on Kenny's.

He looked up.

Their eyes met.

"Play one more hand," she urged.

"Why, so you can clean me out, watch and all?"

"Oh, right. You're a rich man, Mr. Trueblood. I'd bet what you've lost this evening is mere pocket change."

"Then you'd lose that bet, Miss McCellan." Kenny arched an eyebrow in a sardonic expression.

Deannie threw back her head and laughed. "Please, don't pull my leg. I've seen your family

homestead. I'm sure your father left you sitting pretty."

"So that's your game." Kenny nodded. "I figured you were up to something."

"I don't know what you mean."

"Come on, it's obvious the way you play cards you've been hustling us."

She fluttered her eyelashes. "A girl has to make a living. So, are you in or are you out? I take cars, boats, even ranches."

"I hate to tell you this, darlin', but if you're gold diggin', you're barking up the wrong Trueblood. The old man left the whole kit and caboodle to my little brother, Brodie."

BRODIE WAS A HORSE OF A DIFFERENT COLOR.

Deannie gnawed a thumbnail, chewing off her Cherry Delight fingernail polish. She sat in the parking lot outside the Lonesome Dove, over two thousand dollars in cash resting in her lap, but her victory was hollow. No matter how well she played cards, she could never entice Brodie into gambling. She'd sensed that about the man from the moment she'd clapped eyes on him.

The sun dipped toward the western horizon. Long shadows slanted across the parking lot. Car doors slammed and cowboys laughed as more people arrived. Deannie could hear the steady throbbing beat from the jukebox as the front door opened and closed again and again.

What now?

Where did she go from here? Fifteen years of hard work shot straight down the tubes. A lump of emotion dammed her throat at the thought that her plans had been for nothing.

"Rafe Trueblood, you son of a gun, why did you have to die before I got here?" Deannie spoke aloud.

There had to be a way to get to Brodie. If not through gambling, then something else. She would discover his weakness and exploit it because Deannie would not rest until Willow Creek Ranch once more belonged to a Hollis.

But how?

Deannie glimpsed herself in the rearview mirror. To be social, she'd had a beer while playing cards. The alcohol blushed her cheeks with a faint rosy glow. She had repeatedly raked her hand through her hair, and now her auburn tresses tumbled down her shoulders in hedonistic disarray.

Many men had praised her beauty, telling her she looked exactly like a young Nicole Kidman, only shorter, but Deannie had never felt comfortable with her appearance or their compliments.

In her heart, she was still that gawky freckle-faced tomboy in braids. She believed that men, especially Kenny Trueblood types, dished up flattery like candy, hoping to entice gullible females into their beds. Hadn't Daddy warned her to protect her virtue at all costs?

What if she used her looks to attract Brodie Trueblood?

The thought was unexpected but logical. Although Brodie differed greatly from his father and brother, he was still a man. A man who could be charmed by the wiles of a woman determined to get what was hers—Willow Creek Ranch.

"Are you seriously thinking about marrying Brodie Trueblood?" Deannie spoke to her reflection in the mirror.

Because nothing short of marrying him would achieve her goal. A strange sensation raced through her at the thought. Married to that potent male?

Oh my.

She could divorce him later. The judge might give her the ranch in the divorce settlement when he discovered she was really Deanna Hollis, and the ranch was rightfully hers.

Her hands trembled. Did she dare do something so bold?

"It's the only answer." Excitement built inside her. But how did she go about getting Brodie to propose marriage?

She needed a plan. She had to place herself in his vicinity. Repeatedly. How was she going to accomplish that?

Starting her ten-year-old Ford sedan, the only possession her father had left her, Deannie pulled out of the parking lot, her mind racing. Had Brodie gone to the hospital to be with his sister-in-law? Or had he returned home to Willow Creek? Either way, she couldn't go wrong heading toward the ranch.

On her way out of town, Deannie drove through a poverty-stricken part of Rascal. Threading her way through crooked backstreets, she finally found what she was looking for.

A homeless shelter.

Still there after fifteen years. The place where she and Daddy had taken refuge the first night Rafe had thrown them from their home.

Vividly, she remembered the horror of that night, clutching Daddy's hand as he led her here to this dark, scary place that smelled of boiled cabbage and old gym socks. The workers served them overcooked stew and stale cornbread, but it had been food.

She and Daddy had slept together on a mattress on the cement floor. Deannie had sucked her thumb and cried for her pink ruffled canopy bed and her Shetland pony, Hero.

Rafe Trueblood had been responsible. It was all his

fault they were on the streets, and life had never been the same again. That's when her burning hatred had begun.

Fighting back tears, Deannie got out of the car, dashed up the uneven steps in the gathering darkness, and banged on the door. Paint, once white, now a dingy gray, peeled off the side of the building in long strips.

"Yes?" asked the young pregnant woman with a beatific smile who answered her knock. "May I help you?"

"Do you work here?" Deannie asked.

"I'm July Johnson Haynes, the director. Are you in need?" She wrapped her arm around her extended belly.

"No. I want to help." Taking a deep breath, Deannie shoved the money she'd taken from the men at the poker game into the woman's startled hands.

"My goodness, are you sure? This is a lot of money."

But Deannie was already flying down the steps, her breath coming in spurts. She drove away without looking back.

☙❦❧

IT WAS NEAR MIDNIGHT BY THE TIME BRODIE TURNED off the highway and onto the graveled road leading home. A satisfied smile rested on his lips. Emma had done well, bringing another Trueblood into the world. A boy. Philip Brodie. Seven pounds, eight ounces, and in full possession of a great pair of lungs.

And even Kenny had finally shown up, just in time to take Brodie's place in the delivery room. Grudgingly, he gave his older brother credit for that at least.

Yawning, Brodie turned the corner. His headlights reflected off a car parked on the shoulder of the road. The hood was raised.

Brodie slowed, squinting into the darkness. He didn't recognize the car as belonging to a neighbor.

Someone stepped from the shadows.

A woman.

She raised her arms, shielding her eyes against his high-beam lights.

Brodie braked and veered off the road. Leaving his engine idling, he got out. "You all right, ma'am?" he asked as he walked back to her stalled vehicle.

"Thank heavens you stopped," she said, her voice reedy in the cool evening air. She moved toward him. "My cell phone won't hold a charge. I thought I'd be stranded here all night."

"Not too many people live on this road," he said. "Are you visiting someone?" The clouds rolled away from the moon, bathing the road in a silvery shimmer.

The woman tossed her head, her hair tumbling sexily about her shoulders. Her skin glowed ethereally in the gossamer moonlight. She looked like a fairy sprite.

"No." She shook her head, and her curls danced bewitchingly. "I'm afraid I took a wrong turn, and then my car conked out."

Something about her was familiar.

Frowning, Brodie tilted his head. She stood a few feet from him, shivering slightly, her arms crossed over her chest. "Are you cold?"

"A little."

Brodie unbuttoned his flannel shirt, then stripped it off.

"Oh, please, you don't have to give me your shirt."

"No trouble. I've got a T-shirt on underneath." He handed her his shirt.

Tentatively, she shrugged into it. The sleeves dangled way past her hands, giving her a lost-little-girl appearance. "Thank you."

"Do I know you?" He studied her face in the moonlight. They were so close he could smell her scent, sweet as magnolias and twice as nice.

"I'm Deannie McCellan." She extended her hand.

Her palm felt so soft in his. Soft and warm and pleasant.

"Nice to meet you, Miss McCellan. I'm Brodie Trueblood," he said, surprised to find that his words got hung up in his throat.

"Hmm, I think we met, but we weren't formally introduced."

He stared into her eyes, mesmerized. "At the Lonesome Dove this afternoon."

"That's right." She smiled.

Unnerved, Brodie realized he was still holding on to her hand. Embarrassed, he let go and took a step back. "You were with my brother, Kenny."

"I was merely playing cards with him and his friends," she corrected. "I think you got the wrong impression."

"Oh, no...I mean...I didn't think...oh, hell." Brodie swept his cowboy hat off his head. "I didn't mean to imply any relationship between you and Kenny. I was just mad at him."

"No need to apologize." She smiled so brightly Brodie feared he'd melt under the intensity.

"Not meaning to be rude, but why's a lady like you hanging out with guys like my brother and his friends?"

"Everybody has to let off some steam now and then. The fellas invited me to play cards with them, and I thought, what the heck?"

"I see." Except he didn't see at all why a classy woman like her would want to mix with Kenny and his friends. He shifted his weight and settled his hat back on his head. "What seems to be wrong with your car, miss?"

"Please..." she whispered in that sultry voice of hers. "...call me Deannie."

"Deannie."

She shook her head. "I don't know. I'm hopeless with anything mechanical. One minute I was driving along, the next thing I knew the car started to clatter and shake, and it simply stopped."

"Were you able to steer it?"

"No. That's why I'm parked so haphazardly." She indicated the car with a wave.

"Could be the drive shaft," Brodie mused, stroking his jaw with a thumb and forefinger.

"Is that bad?"

"It's not good."

Deannie sighed. "Oh, my. I hope it doesn't cost a lot. I have little money."

"The fellas at the bar clean you out?"

She ducked her head.

"I don't mean to tell you how to run your business, but gambling is a habit that only leads to trouble."

"I don't indulge often." She batted her eyelashes at him, and Brodie had the strangest feeling that Deannie McCellan was gambling right at that moment.

"That comment was outta line; I don't know you. But my daddy was a professional gambler, and my brother seems to have followed in his footsteps. I know firsthand how ruinous gambling can be."

"I appreciate your concern, but I can take care of myself."

Was she making fun of him? It was hard to read her expression in the dim moonlight, but her voice took on a teasing tone.

"I could look at your car tonight, but truthfully, it would be better to wait until morning. One of my ranch hands is also a mechanic. He could probably fix it for the cost of parts."

"Do you really think so? That would be great."

"Is there someone I can call for you?" Brodie asked, disturbed by his attraction to this woman.

"I know no one in this part of the country. I was on my way to a job interview in Santa Fe."

"I see." So, she was unemployed?

Watch out, Brodie, the voice in the back of his head warned. *There's something not quite right about this gorgeous filly. She's not at all what she seems.*

"Yeah, I sound like a security risk. No job, no money, a faulty cell phone, and a broken-down car." Deannie laughed.

The rich, throaty sound affected Brodie viscerally, catching him low in the belly. "You can stay at my ranch. I've got an empty guest room, and you're more than welcome. We'll worry about the car first thing tomorrow morning."

"That's so generous of you, but I can't possibly put you out like that." She pursed her full lips, and it bothered Brodie that he couldn't seem to take his eyes off that sweet mouth. "What would your wife say about you bringing home a stranger?"

"I'm not married."

"Handsome fellow like you? How come?"

"Guess I've never found the right one."

"Hmm." She tapped her chin with an index finger. "I suppose that's an even stronger reason for me to decline your kind invitation. We wouldn't want to set local tongues wagging, would we? You've got to live here."

"Don't worry about that. The Truebloods keep the Presidio County gossips in business. We're more reliable than Facebook."

Deannie smiled. "Well, if you're sure."

"It's no problem."

"Then I accept."

Her acceptance felt like a gift, and it shouldn't have. Why had he asked her to stay? Was he insane? Tempting fate like this? She'd been hanging out in a bar with Kenny for heaven's sake. Brodie couldn't deny his attraction to her, but common sense cautioned him not to get tangled up with this woman.

But what else could he do? He wasn't about to leave her here all night. It was twenty miles back to Rascal, and he had to be up at five. She would stay one night. No big deal. Rory would fix her car tomorrow, and she would be on her way. End of story. He need never explore this unexpected fascination with Deannie McCellan.

"Let me get my bag from the car," she said.

Brodie waited while she opened the trunk and retrieved a duffel bag and her purse.

"All set." She grinned, reappearing at his elbow, her intoxicating magnolia fragrance filling his nose and making him think of white lace wedding gowns and diamond engagement rings.

Swallowing hard, Brodie escorted her to the passenger side of his pickup truck, pondering the sudden acceleration of his pulse.

He unlocked the door and put out a hand to help her up. Being a gentleman, he hadn't even thought about it, but the second his hand touched her skin, he felt an electrical spark that lit him up inside.

Quickly, he stepped away. He wasn't sure, but he thought he heard her catch her breath.

Sliding behind the wheel, he put the truck in gear and headed for home. They drove in silence. Brodie cleared his throat, racking his brain for something to say.

"So," Deannie said, "did Kenny's wife have her baby?"

"Yes." Brodie smiled. "Another boy. Phillip Brodie."

"She named him after you?"

"It was nice of her."

"I'm sure you deserve the honor."

"I don't know about that."

"I am. Any man that is gallant enough to rescue a bar dolly with a broken-down car in the middle of the night is a true gentleman."

"I'm sorry about that 'bar dolly' crack." Grateful for the cover of darkness, Brodie felt his face flame.

"Believe me, people have called me much worse," Deannie assured him.

"That would never happen around me." The idea of someone verbally abusing her sent anger coursing through his whole system. Why did he feel so protective of her?

"You're a true gentleman."

Brodie squirmed in his seat. "Guess I'm sort of old-fashioned."

"I find it refreshing."

Up ahead, Brodie spotted the security lights of Willow Creek. He'd never been so glad to see the place in his entire life.

"Here we are," he said, turning into the long driveway.

Deannie pressed her face against the window, and he could have sworn her breath quickened.

"All this is yours?"

"Yep. My father died two weeks ago and left the ranch to me. But I've been running it for years. If I hadn't taken it over, the old man would have bankrupted the place away years ago."

"Not good with money, was he?"

Brodie sighed. "Not good with much of anything."

"That must have been tough."

"Yeah, well, we all got troubles, right?" They bumped along the dirt road, ambling over the cattle guard and through the big gate.

"You're very lucky," she said.

Was that sarcasm in her voice? Was she jealous? She

had no right to be. He'd earned everything he'd achieved through hard, honest work.

"Willow Creek is my life."

Deannie's face turned away from him, but he noticed her shoulders stiffened.

"Like I said," she murmured, "you're lucky."

"I love nothing the way I love this land," he said.

"I can understand that feeling," she said, her words muffled.

"Can you?" Brodie pulled up in front of the house and killed the engine. He looked over at her, but she didn't answer him.

Their eyes met, and an odd tension stretched between them. It felt too intimate. Brodie gulped, confused.

"C'mon in," he said, "I'll show you to your room."

4

Curiously, Deannie's heart slowed until she feared it might stop beating altogether. After fifteen years, she'd finally come home.

Following Brodie through the back door and into the kitchen, she fought the assault of memories tumbling through her mind. Her vision narrowed, and the past rushed at her hard.

She remembered many times running in and out of that same door until her mama, pressing Daddy's shirts at the ironing board, hollered at her to come inside or stay outside. They weren't paying to cool the whole outdoors.

And the kitchen!

When Brodie flicked on the overhead light, Deannie sucked in her breath at the shock of seeing it again. The color of the walls was different and so were the furnishings, but it was the kitchen she'd known. She had sat in that spot by the bay window and eaten her breakfast, watching birds at the feeder in the mesquite tree.

Her mother had washed Deannie's hair in that sink, had baked cookies in that oven, had stocked canned goods in that pantry. Deannie even fancied she could smell Mama's clean, wholesome scent, a combination of soap, peaches, and homemade bread.

Blood drained from her face, and she suddenly felt freezing. She hugged herself. Perspiration dampened her forehead, and she feared she might faint.

"Deannie?"

Brodie's voice came to her from a fog. She shook her head.

His arm went around her waist, strong but gentle. "Are you all right?" His mouth was close to her ear. Too close. He sounded worried. "Here, sit down."

Obediently, she sank into the chair he pulled out for her.

"Have you eaten today?"

"Peanuts. At the bar," she murmured, surprised at how weak her limbs felt.

"And I suppose you were drinking, too."

Was that judgment she heard in his voice? "Just one beer."

"On an empty stomach." He clicked his tongue and turned his back to rummage through the refrigerator. "Actually, I got so wrapped up in coaching Emma through her labor, I didn't eat supper, either. Matilda will hit the roof, but we're raiding the fridge."

"Matilda?"

Brodie had said he wasn't married, but what if he had a live-in girlfriend? An emotion, curiously like jealousy, stabbed through her. Surely, she wasn't jealous. How could she be jealous? No, she was just worried about complications. Getting rid of a girlfriend would add to the complexity of her scheme.

"Matilda Jennings is my housekeeper."

"And she gets mad when you raid your own refrigerator?"

"Matilda's not one for cleaning up other people's messes."

"Then why do you keep her on as a housekeeper?"

"Out here, housekeepers aren't so easy to come by. With Emma and the kids, I need all the help I can get, but ever since they moved in, Matilda's been testy." He chuckled.

"At least you have a sense of humor about it."

Brodie shrugged. "I can't see any other way to approach the situation."

He hauled out a platter of roast beef, sliced purple onions, a jar of mayonnaise, lettuce, tomatoes, pickles, and olives. Retrieving a loaf of whole wheat from the breadbasket on the counter, he set the food on the table.

Stomach growling, Deannie watched as he made sandwiches and poured two glasses of milk.

"Try that," he said, sliding a plate in front of her.

Deannie sank her teeth into the sandwich. It tasted like heaven. Just the kind of hearty rustic sandwiches her mother used to make. "Oh my."

Brodie winked. "I think we have chocolate chip cookies for dessert."

"Are you trying to seduce me?" she joked. "Because chocolate chip cookies will do it."

"No roses and wine for you?"

"I've got a sweet tooth."

"You don't say."

"Yep. Crazy for red velvet cake and cherry pie too."

"I'll keep that in mind."

Deannie met his gaze and stopped chewing. She was wearing his shirt, and it smelled of him, the soft material rubbing against her skin. It was as if he had enveloped her in a massive bear hug.

Under the scrutiny of bright lights, the man was even more handsome than she'd imagined. He possessed a long, firm jawline and a straight nose. He doffed his cowboy hat and settled it into the chair beside him. A ridge ringed his dark hair where the hat left its imprint. He smiled at her, and his brown eyes crinkled at the corners.

Something tugged deep within her, something dangerous and exciting.

They both dropped their gazes at the same time.

Get a grip.

His handsomeness would make winning his affections less odious, but she must never forget he was a Trueblood. She'd come to Willow Creek with a mission —win back her family home. If she couldn't gamble the place out from under Kenny, then she would seduce it out of Brodie.

But she would have to be darned careful not to lose her heart in the bargain. He was too hot for her own good.

"That was delicious," she said, wiping her hands on a paper napkin. "Thank you."

"You're welcome." He ducked his head, looking shy, and gathered up the food. "About those cookies..."

"I was worried you'd forgotten."

"Not a chance."

He opened the cookie jar on the counter and fished out two oversized chocolate chip cookies, then handed one to her along with another paper napkin for catching the crumbs and sat down beside her to enjoy his cookie.

A piece of cobweb she hadn't noticed before was stuck in his hair. He must have run into it in the dark with his cowboy hat and when he'd taken off his hat, the sticky web had attached to his lush locks. Deannie raised her hand, almost touching his head.

He gave her the side-eye. "What is it?"

"Cobweb in your hair." She hadn't intended on touching him, but his hair was so thick and silky and black as a raven's wing. She brushed the web away with her fingertips.

"Matilda thinks I should spray for pests." He winked. "But I'm a live-and-let-live kind of guy. Plus, spiders are beneficial."

Deannie concentrated on her cookie. He'd done it again. Treating her as if he cared about her. The man was open, warm, and welcoming.

He dusted his fingers and stood to collect their dirty dishes.

"Let me help you with that." Scraping back her chair, she got up too.

"We can just dump the dirty plates in the sink."

"And risk making Matilda mad?"

"It's too late at night to be worrying about washing dishes," Brodie took the plates from her hands.

Their fingers brushed lightly.

Brodie jumped back as if scalded, dropping a plate to the floor. It shattered, sending splinters flying across the hardwood floor, and he swore softly under his breath.

"I'll get the broom," Deannie said, and without thinking, stepped into the anteroom and opened the broom closet. She turned around to find Brodie standing behind her.

"How did you know where the broom closet was?"

"Lucky guess." Whew, boy, she would have to watch herself. She hadn't thought twice, heading instinctively for the broom closet. Another stupid mistake like that one and she would tip her hand for sure. "A lot of these old farmhouses have similar floor plans."

Brodie said nothing, but suddenly a suspicious gleam lit his eyes, and all his open warmth closed up like a clamshell. He pressed his lips firmly together. Taking the broom and dustpan from her, he silently swept up the glass.

"I'll show you to your room," he said, dumping the glass in the trash can and returning the utensils to the broom closet.

Deannie gathered up her duffel bag and purse and followed Brodie upstairs. The hallway was lit by a series of night-lights. The old floorboards creaked under their weight. It looked like home, and yet, it was not.

The Truebloods had carved their mark in her family homestead. The wall color was different, as was the carpeting. And the house smelled of Brodie—masculine, outdoorsy—leather and hay and sunshine.

What was he thinking? Deannie fretted, watching

his shoulders sway. His mood had changed so quickly in the kitchen. Why?

He led her past the master bedroom where her parents used to sleep. Her old room was next door. But Brodie didn't stop there. He took her down the hall to the last bedroom on the right.

"You'll be comfortable here," he said rather stiffly. "Now, if you'll excuse me, I'm going to bed. I've got to be up in four hours."

"Yes. Thanks."

Turning, he sauntered back toward the master bedroom.

Deannie opened the door and switched on the light. This had once been her mother's quilting room. The sewing machine had stood near the window where a full-size oak bedroom suite now sat. Mom had spent many hours here making quilts. Stacks of material, boxes of thread, yards of lace and ribbon had decorated the shelf that now held books and various knickknacks.

Fierce nostalgia swept through her. A vivid longing for what used to be. She owed it to herself, to her parents, to reclaim what was rightfully hers. Her memories were here, her history, her past.

Her future.

Changing from Brodie's work shirt and her silky dress into a blue cotton nightgown, Deannie padded across the hall to the bathroom where she brushed her teeth and washed the makeup from her face. Once finished, she returned to her bedroom, shut the door, and slipped between the cool sheets.

Her body was tired, but her mind raced, fully alert. Disabling her car on the roadside had been a stroke of genius. Thank heavens no one else had driven by before Brodie.

The plot had worked wonderfully. The stalled vehicle had gotten her in the door; now it was up to her to turn up the heat under the sizzle that Lady Luck had created between the two.

Coming home to Willow Creek, seeing the ranch again after fifteen years, solidified her resolve. She had to get her home back. And if that meant she would have to marry Brodie Trueblood to accomplish her goals, then that's what she would do.

Deannie could think of far worse fates than being married to that gorgeous hunk of man.

❦

HAD DEANNIE LIED ABOUT HER ASSOCIATION WITH Kenny?

Brodie rolled over in bed, cupped the back of his head in his palms, and stared at the ceiling. How had she known where the broom closet was? Had she and Kenny been using the farmhouse as their trysting place whenever he was away?

Cringing at the thought of his brother and Deannie having an illicit affair in one of these bedrooms, Brodie bit down on his bottom lip to stifle a groan. He hated to believe it, but the truth was he'd found her in a bar playing poker with Kenny. That didn't speak well of her character.

Judge not, least ye be judged.

His mother's favorite biblical quote floated through his head. How many times had she recited that phrase when he'd railed against his father's reprehensible behavior? Even on her deathbed, the woman had never uttered a condemning word. Brodie was not so forgiving. From his viewpoint, his father was a scoundrel.

But what about Deannie?

Was it pure coincidence she'd made a wrong turn and her car had stalled on the road to Willow Creek? Or had she been hoping to rendezvous with Kenny? Had his brother kissed those full sweet lips right here in this house? Had his hands caressed Deannie's skin, kneaded her breasts? Oh, God! Why did the thought burn his gut, tighten his chest?

Because he didn't want to see Kenny treating Emma the way his father had treated his mother. That was why. He felt no jealousy. None. How could he be jealous when he didn't even know the woman?

Yet, there was something about Deannie. The calm serenity in those pale-blue eyes, the sheen of her auburn hair, the regal way she carried herself, captured his imagination the way no woman had in a long time.

When they had been in the kitchen together, eating sandwiches, he'd had the most overpowering urge to lean over and kiss her. Merely brushing her fingertips had caused him o drop that plate.

Could it be he was just eager for a relationship, and Deannie was in the right place at the right time?

Sighing, Brodie flopped over onto his side.

No. It was more than that. He felt an odd emotion he couldn't explain. Something he'd never really experienced before. Something that told him she might be the one he'd been waiting for.

Proceed with caution, Trueblood. No point jumping the gun.

Especially when his heart was on the line. The last thing he needed was to get mixed up with a female version of his father.

5

The aroma of strong coffee tugged open Deannie's eyelids at six a.m. Habit urged her to roll over and go back to sleep, but one name popped into her mind, settling the issue.

Brodie.

Flinging the covers aside, Deannie sat up. She had to make the most of the morning. As soon as Brodie's ranch hand inspected her car and discovered nothing wrong with it, she would have no excuse for lingering at Willow Creek. Time was of the essence.

Never an early riser, she yawned, stretched, and rubbed her eyes. "Come on, Deannie, get it in gear," she mumbled.

Changing into jeans and a red cotton blouse, she took a deep breath to fortify herself before putting on sneakers and heading downstairs. She had no idea what her next move would be, but she was good at adapting and thinking on the fly.

Childish voices drifted from the kitchen.

"When's Mama comin' home, Unc' Brodie?"

"This afternoon." Brodie's voice sent shivers skipping down Deannie's spine. The man had the sexiest voice on the planet.

"Thank heavens," a woman muttered.

"With our new baby brother?" the child chirped.

"Uh-huh."

Deannie peeked around the corner into the kitchen. A tall, middle-aged woman stood at the sink scrubbing dishes, her steel-gray curls shaking with movement, her mouth pressed into a hard, uncompromising line.

Brodie sat at the table, two children in his lap. Tucked in the crook of his left arm was a blond girl of about three. The boy, slightly older and the spitting image of Kenny, nestled on his right.

"Who's her?" The little boy pointed a finger at Deannie.

"Probably the one who messed up my kitchen last night." The woman at the sink turned to glare at Deannie. No doubt this was the infamous Matilda.

"Good morning," Brodie greeted her, a smile on his face. "Come have breakfast with us."

Deannie returned his smile and wriggled her fingers.

"Yeah, come on in." Matilda heaved a sigh. "Doesn't matter that I just got through feeding the ranch hands."

"Matilda, Miss McCellan is our guest. I trust you'll remember that," Brodie admonished the surly housekeeper.

"Don't go to any trouble. Cereal is fine with me," Deannie said.

"Good," Matilda huffed. "Cornflakes are in the pantry."

Feeling like a pariah, Deannie inched past Matilda, took cornflakes from the pantry, a bowl from the cupboard, and milk from the refrigerator, then settled in across the table from Brodie and the kids.

"You pretty," the girl announced. "Whatcha name?"

"I'm Deannie, and you're beautiful."

The little girl beamed. "I knowed."

Deannie grinned at the girl.

"I wike you red hair."

"I like your golden hair."

The child giggled. They had a mutual admiration society going on here.

"This is Angel," Brodie said, affectionately tweaking the child's ear. "And this one here is Richard, but we all call him Buster."

"Hi," Deannie said. She hadn't been around children much and wasn't sure how to deal with them, but she had a feeling if she could charm the little tikes, she might melt Uncle Brodie's heart.

And melting Brodie Trueblood's heart was number one on her to-do list.

"Sleep well?" Brodie asked, handing Angel a piece of diamond shaped toast.

"Not long enough." Deannie suppressed a yawn. "I'm afraid I'm not much of an early bird."

"You wazy bones!" Angel pointed a finger at her and laughed.

"Yes, that's me. Lazy bones."

"Maybe try not spending so much time in bars," Brodie said.

Was he teasing or warning her? Deannie wasn't sure.

She studied his face. "You're right, a girl can pick up some very bad habits in those places."

"How bad?" he asked, eyes twinkling.

Okay, very definitely teasing. Their gazes welded.

Brodie didn't blink.

Deannie gulped.

"This job you're applying for in New Mexico, is it in a bar?" he asked.

Deannie had almost forgotten about the white lie she'd told him the night before about a job in New Mexico. She pretended to look ashamed, still teasing. "Guilty as charged."

Brodie nodded. "I'll tow your car into the yard. Whenever Rory can spare a few minutes from his regular chores this morning, he'll take a look at it."

"Thank you."

"I suppose you'd like to be on your way as soon as possible."

Was that a hint? Did he want her gone? Well, too bad, she wasn't giving up that easily. "No hurry," she said lightly. "I wouldn't want to cause an inconvenience."

"Hop up, kids, I've got work to do." Brodie eased Angel and Buster from his lap. Getting to his feet, he took his straw cowboy hat from a peg on the wall and settled it onto his head.

He cut a dashing figure. The epitome of a West Texas cowboy, in his faded jeans and well-worn work boots. He looked like he belonged at Willow Creek.

That idea startled Deannie.

Truthfully, she'd never thought beyond getting even with Rafe Trueblood, but she had to consider that Brodie might love this ranch as much as she did. She studied his muscled forearms peeking from beneath rolled-up shirtsleeves. His top two shirt buttons lay undone, and she could see tufts of sexy black hair.

He'd started out the door just as the landline phone rang. In the Trans-Pecos, cell phones were unreliable, and everyone kept a landline.

Matilda answered, then called to him. "It's for you."

Treading back across the room, he favored Deannie with another whiff of his deliciously masculine scent. This morning he smelled of soap and bacon, toothpaste and coffee.

Deannie took a bite of cornflakes and tried not to notice.

"Hello?" he spoke into the cordless receiver.

She didn't mean to eavesdrop, but she was sitting right at Brodie's elbow. Short of clamping her hands over her ears, she had to listen to his side of the conversation.

"Emma. How are you and the baby this morning?"

"It's Mama!" Buster exclaimed, jumping up and down. "I wanna talk."

"Me too, me too," Angel squealed.

"Emma, why are you crying?" A concerned expression folded Brodie's mouth into a straight line. "Calm down, I can't understand you."

"Mama," Buster whined, reaching for the phone.

Deannie placed an index finger to her lip. "Shh," she whispered to Buster. "Let Uncle Brodie talk to your mama."

Buster stared at her. "No!" he announced, wrapping his arms around his uncle's leg and burying his face against his hip.

Nice try, Brodie mouthed at Deannie.

She had a sudden urge to slink off into the corner for stirring up more problems by trying to help.

"Is Kenny there?" Brodie asked his sister-in-law. Apparently, Emma answered in the negative because Brodie turned his head and swore softly under his breath. "What's that? An infection? I'm sorry, Emma. How much longer will you be in the hospital?"

"Oh, no," Matilda erupted, throwing her hands into the air. "I'm not taking care of these brats any longer. It's not my job."

"Is the baby okay?" he asked Emma and made slicing motions at Matilda, indicating she needed to hush. "Good. Don't worry about Buster and Angel. I'll hold down the fort."

"I mean it." Matilda threw down the kitchen towel she was using to wipe down the counter. "I didn't sign on for this."

Glaring at Matilda, Brodie bent down and scooped a sobbing Buster into his arms as he held the phone tucked between his shoulder and his ear.

Matilda clanged a pan against the sink for emphasis.

Tears drizzled down Angel's cheeks. "Mommy, Mommy. Where's my mommy?"

Poor Brodie. He had an irresponsible brother on the loose, a hysterical sister-in-law on the phone, two crying kids clinging to him, and a witchy housekeeper dishing out grief. For the first time in her life, Deannie felt sorry for a Trueblood.

"Those kids need a good hard spanking," Matilda groused. "That'll straighten 'em right up."

"Here, Buster, talk to your mama." Face flushed,

Brodie handed the phone to his nephew and set him on the bar stool.

Whirling on his heels, he stalked across the kitchen to confront Matilda. "You're fired," he said.

Matilda crossed her arms over her chest. "Fine with me. You've been impossible to please ever since your sister-in-law and those kids moved in here."

"Out!" he thundered, pointing a finger at the door. "You've got four hours to collect your things and be gone."

With a toss of her head, Matilda sailed out of the room.

Slumping down in the chair beside Deannie, Brodie lowered his head and plowed fingers through his hair. "What am I going to do now?" he muttered. "I've got a ranch to run. I don't have time to watch two preschoolers."

Fate had dropped a plum into her lap. Last night's emergency plan with the stalled car had only been a temporary solution. This current situation, however, offered her a prime opportunity to be close to Brodie for another day or two. Long enough to fuel his interest in her.

Deannie cleared her throat.

Brodie raised his eyes.

Steepling her fingers, Deannie took a deep breath and a calculated risk. "I'll be happy to watch the kids and keep house for you until your sister-in-law is out of the hospital."

No. Definitely not. Bad idea. A disaster waiting to happen.

Brodie knew he could not stay under the same roof with this bewitching woman for the next two or three days completely unchaperoned except for children. Plus, he knew absolutely nothing about Deannie save for the fact she turned him on, and for all he knew, she could be his brother's mistress.

He stared at Deannie.

Was that why she wanted the job? To get closer to Kenny? Did she think by playing nursemaid to his kids, she would worm her way into his brother's heart, and he would divorce his wife? If that was her plan, she was way off beam. Kenny rarely put in an appearance at Willow Creek. In fact, he hadn't been around since Rafe's funeral, when Emma and the kids had moved in.

Deannie's eyes, the pale blue of the morning sky, widened, and he felt like a jerk for being so suspicious.

"Just an offer," she said lightly.

"I...er...well," Brodie stammered, unsure of how to refuse her. He wanted to say yes, but what did he really know about Deannie?

"I want down," Buster hollered from the bar stool. "Mama hung up."

Brodie got to his feet, grateful for the distraction, and put Buster on the floor. Settling the telephone receiver back in its cradle, he glanced over and saw Angel standing in a chair, her fingers in the butter dish.

"Oh, no." He groaned as she stuck a handful of butter into her mouth. "Angel, stop that."

"I wike butter." His niece gave him a greasy yellow smile.

Brodie swung his gaze to Deannie. She sat with her hands folded demurely in her lap, a serene expression on her face. Ha! These two hellions would erase that smile from her lips in nothing flat.

"You're hired." Brodie reached for Angel. "Could you start right away?"

OKAY, SO SHE WASN'T ALL THAT DOMESTIC. THAT didn't mean she was helpless. Did it? Deannie glanced at the two wide-eyed children staring at her. What now? No wonder Brodie had looked relieved when he'd headed out the back door.

Oh well, nothing to do but roll up her sleeves and plunge right in.

If she wanted to convince Brodie she was the marrying kind, she would have to prove she could manage a house and kids.

"What do you guys usually do after breakfast?" she asked.

"Video games!" Buster giggled.

"P'ay in mud!" Angel squealed.

Three and five years old and already con artists. No denying these two were Truebloods.

"You ever play hide-and-seek?"

"Yeah!" Buster wriggled his little hips with excitement.

"No." Angel shook her head.

"Yes, you have, 'member?" Buster scoffed.

"Nuh-uh."

He shoved his sister. Angel slugged him with a tiny fist.

"Now, now. No hitting." Deannie stepped between them. "If you don't play nice, it's naptime for both of you."

"You can't make us." Buster defiantly folded his chubby arms across his chest, lowered his chin, and glared at her.

"Yeah. You not our mama." Angel backed her brother.

"Your Uncle Brodie left me in charge. So whatever I say goes. If you're nice to me, I'll be nice to you. If not..."

"What?" Buster challenged.

Yeah, Deannie, what?

"Wet's p'ay hide-and-seek," Angel wheedled, pushing blond curls from her face. "Kay, Buster?"

Buster relaxed his stance and dropped his arms. "Okay."

"Let's go upstairs to play," Deannie urged. She was dying to get a peek in Brodie's room. The bedroom that had once belonged to her parents.

Once they were upstairs, Deannie said, "This chair in the hall is base. I'll sit here, close my eyes, and count to one hundred while you guys go hide. You've got to stay hidden until I come looking for you. Then you try to get back to base before I tag you. Understand?"

Angel nodded.

"Yeah, yeah, I know how to play." Buster looked bored.

"All set?" Deannie eased herself down in the chair

and put her hands over her eyes. "One, two, three, four..."

Giggles and the sound of running feet.

The minute they dispersed, Deannie got to her feet and headed for Brodie's bedroom. "Ten, eleven, hide real good..." she sang out, her heart suddenly racing as her hand closed over the doorknob.

"Twelve, thirteen..." She pushed into the bedroom.

Brodie kept the place exceptionally tidy. No clothes on the floor, no overflowing wastebaskets, no dirty dishes. A bookcase housed a variety of fiction and nonfiction titles. Cowboy paintings decorated one wall. A small writing desk sat in one corner with a laptop computer perched on top.

She hadn't really expected to see anything remaining that had once belonged to her parents, but the sight of the huge, four-poster oak bed was Deannie's undoing.

Her breath caught in her lungs.

A flash of memory shot through her mind. Suddenly she was Buster's age, padding into the room in her pajamas. Mama and Daddy were snuggling together beneath the down quilt. They spotted her and threw back the covers, inviting her to join them. Joy had surged through her as she leaped into the family bed and felt her parents' love surround her.

Deannie gulped. Her face flushed alternately hot, then cold. Tears stung her eyelids. Oh, what she had lost! Her mother. Her father. Her home.

And it was Rafe's fault. If he had been there at that very moment, Deannie would have launched herself at him, attacking him with her bare fists.

"Deannie?" She heard Buster's voice calling to her

through the fog enveloping her mind. "You didn't come looking for us."

"That's 'cause she's too busy snooping around in your uncle's bedroom," Matilda said from the doorway, two suitcases clutched in her hands.

Deannie blinked and stared at the angry woman. "The children and I were playing hide-and-seek."

"Don't think I can't see what you're up to," Matilda challenged, setting down the suitcases and sinking her hands on her hips. "Brodie might be a fool, but I ain't."

Deannie bristled. "Don't you dare call him a fool."

"Why not? He's acting like one."

"Brodie fired you. I offered to watch the kids in exchange for having my car repaired. That's all," Deannie said, but deep inside her heart, Matilda's words struck terror. Would she tell Brodie that she'd caught Deannie snooping in his bedroom to get her job back?

Matilda's eyes narrowed. "I know your type. Always scheming. You got your ways. And don't think I will not be keeping an eye on you, because I am. There's something off about you."

"I believe you were headed out the front door," Deannie said.

"Aren't we gonna play anymore?" Buster demanded.

"Yes, honey, we are." Deannie turned her back on the woman, trying her best to ignore the frantic tripping of her pulse. She took Buster's hand. "Come on, let's go find your sister."

Matilda snorted, picked up her suitcases, and headed for the door. Before she flounced out it, she called, "You ain't seen the last of me, little Miss Gold Digger."

6

"What's wrong with the car?" Brodie asked Rory Beam, reining in his horse, Ranger, and sliding off the roan's broad back. Tilting his cowboy hat back on his head, he mopped his brow with a bandana, then tied Ranger to the corral gate.

Rory shook his head. "It's the darnedest thing, boss. Can't find a thing amiss."

"Nothing?"

"Starts fine. I took it up and down the road a few times, no problems."

Brodie angled a look up at the ranch house perched on the hill and pursed his lips. He hated to jump to conclusions, but something about Deannie didn't ring true. The fact Rory could find nothing wrong with her car deepened Brodie's worry that the woman had finagled an overnight invitation to Willow Creek and had ensconced herself in the house until Emma's return so she could be near Kenny.

But was that really fair? He was the one who'd fired Matilda.

Was he attributing Deannie with motives she didn't possess? The part of him that was attracted to her wanted to trust her, but he'd been through too much in his life to not question her motives.

It was time he had a heart-to-heart with his brother and find out just what was going on between him and this woman.

"I'm headed into town," Brodie told Rory.

"Okay."

"Keep checking out her car. I'd hate to have the thing die on Deannie halfway between here and Santa Fe."

"Will do." Rory nodded and wiped his grease-stained hands on a red rag pulled from his pocket and went back to work.

Half an hour later, Brodie found Kenny at the Lonesome Dove pitching darts.

"Do you ever go home?" he asked his older brother.

"Now and then, when I need a fresh change of clothes." Kenny landed a bull's-eye.

"Did you hear about Emma's complications?"

"Yeah. I dropped by the hospital an hour ago."

"Well, bully for you. Have you given any thought to seeing your kids?"

Kenny looked chagrined. "I guess I need to do that."

"Damned straight you do."

"Okay, I'll come by and pick them up this evening."

"Is that the only reason you'd be coming to Willow Creek?" Brodie glanced sideways at his brother and realized he was hoping against hope Kenny would deny any involvement with Deannie. Would he believe him if he did?

"What are you talking about?" Kenny threw another dart.

"Your mistress." Brodie pressed his lips tightly together, trying his best to ignore the knot growing in his gut.

"My *what*?"

"Don't try to deny it."

"Little brother, I don't have a clue what you're talking about."

"Deannie McCellan."

"Who's that?"

"The woman you played cards with last night."

"Oh yeah, the redhead."

"Yes. Her. You're telling me you and she don't have a thing going on?"

"Come on, little brother, I have my faults, but I've never cheated on Emma."

"You think I'm going to buy that? You live just like Rafe. Gambling, drinking, hanging out with lowlifes. You expect me to believe you didn't inherit his womanizing genes, too?"

"I don't have to listen to your crap. You come struttin' in here all high and mighty and expect me to explain myself to you. Just because you like taking the moral high ground doesn't mean you're always right. There's nothing wrong with having a good time."

Brodie clenched his fists and willed himself not to raise their age-old philosophical differences. "Kenny, tell me the truth. Are you or aren't you having an affair with Deannie? Is that the real reason Emma left?"

"I ain't denying I've made a lot of mistakes in my marriage, but I love my wife."

"You sure have a funny way of showing it."

"Well, dammit, Brodie, you see how she nags. Always trying to change me."

"With good reason."

Kenny shrugged. "Believe what you want, but I'm telling you I've never cheated on Emma."

"Then what's Deannie doing at Willow Creek?"

"Who knows? It's got nothing to do with me. Maybe she decided you were the better catch."

"What's that supposed to mean?" Alarm skittered up and down his spine. "Do you think she's after me?"

"How would I know?" Kenny glared. "You're the one who popped up accusing me of things I've never done and with a woman I only met once. Why don't you ask *her* what she's doing at Willow Creek?"

Stunned, Brodie stared at his brother. Maybe Deannie's story was true. Maybe her car really had broken down. Maybe she had been on her way to New Mexico for a job interview. Suddenly he felt stupid for doubting her, and curiously, his heart lightened.

All the way back to the ranch, Brodie pondered his blossoming feelings for Deannie. She created a burning excitement in him without even trying. From the moment he'd seen her in the bar, something inside him had clicked.

And this morning, fresh from her bed, sheet wrinkles still creased into her otherwise flawless skin, and offering to take care of the house and kids, she'd triggered a reaction in him.

Everything about her haunted him—her rich, sweet,

intoxicating scent, that long red mane flowing about her slender shoulders, those deep eyes that seemed to stare straight into his soul. That tight little tushy, her soft round breasts, those heavenly legs. He couldn't remember when a woman had interested him this much.

He parked the pickup in the driveway, got out, and went into the house.

Toys littered the kitchen floor. An open package of cookies rested on the cabinet. In the living room, the television droned.

"Deannie?" Brodie called, his gaze sweeping the chaos. "Buster? Angel?"

When he received no answer, Brodie walked up the stairs. Where were they?

"Deannie?" he repeated, pushing open the door to the guest bedroom.

Her duffel bag rested in the middle of the unmade bed, her socks rolled into a ball on the floor. The shirt he'd given her to wear the night before was folded neatly across the back of a chair.

Brodie moved on to the bedroom that Angel and Buster had been sharing since Emma had left Kenny. What he saw had him smiling.

Deannie was sitting in the rocking chair, Angel and Buster cradled in her lap. All three were sound asleep; a picture book lay open in Deannie's lap.

A strange melty feeling settled in his chest as he watched them sleep, a foreign sensation he could find no name for.

Hunger. Longing. The words popped into his head.

Naming the feeling didn't ease his anxiety. In fact, it

spurred the fear buried deep inside him. As much as he might yearn for a family, it terrified him that he could end up like his parents or Kenny and Emma's tattered marriage. He knew nothing about how normal, healthy family dynamics worked. Nothing at all.

That's why he'd thrown himself into making Willow Creek the best ranch it could be. But now that he'd achieved his goal, what came next? Who was it all for?

Recently, however, as his peers paired off and started getting married... His cousin, retired bull rider, Kael Carmody reuniting with his high school sweetheart, Daisy Hightower, and claiming the son he never knew he'd fathered. Watching his friend, software whiz kid turned rancher, Kurt McNally find his ideal mate in legal secretary, Bonnie Bradford, be so happy together. Serving best man to his neighbor, Detective Nick Nickerson as he married his coworker, Michele Prescott. It had unearthed a hole so deep inside Brodie he feared could never be filled.

Kael, Kurt, and Nick had changed after finding love. Growing calmer. More focused. Balanced. They knew when to work and when to play. Their priorities had shifted, and damn if Brodie didn't want that too.

But maybe a family just wasn't in the cards for him. If he was smart, he'd be happy with what he had. His life was good. He was grateful. It was greedy to yearn for more.

Brodie didn't have the heart to wake her and tell her he expected her to cook dinner for six hungry ranch hands.

Instead, he tiptoed downstairs, took the last of the roast beef from the refrigerator, and made sandwiches.

Whistling to himself, Brodie realized, even though he couldn't rightly say why, that he felt more optimistic than he had in a very long time.

LIKE SHOOTING FISH IN A BARREL, DEANNIE THOUGHT the following day, slanting Brodie a glance.

He was looking at her as if she were a delicious confection, his eyes bright and shining, his expression one of moonstruck delight.

She'd changed into skimpy denim shorts and a white halter top, hoping for this exact effect. If she had known winning him over would be this easy, she would never have bothered learning to play poker.

They were standing in the front yard appraising her vehicle while Buster and Angel fed sugar cubes to Brodie's horse, tied beside a weeping willow tree. The breeze rustled through the leaves, cooling Deannie's sunbaked skin.

"Rory couldn't find anything wrong with your car, but that doesn't mean it won't act up on you again," Brodie said. "He said it needed lots of maintenance work. Oil change, fuel filter, spark plugs. When was the last time you had it serviced?"

Deannie shrugged. "I don't remember."

A soft smile curled his lips. "I know it might not be the sort of thing you think about, but vehicle maintenance is important."

Normally, she would have bristled at such a remark, as if he assumed that she knew nothing about taking care of her car just because estrogen pumped through her veins, but under the circumstances, it was perfect. He was playing right into her hands, perceiving her as a helpless female.

And boy was she going to play the role to the hilt. Wooing Brodie Trueblood was like shooting plentiful fish in a tiny barrel. But then again, how many times had her father uttered that same clichéd phrase when betting on a "sure thing" only to have his misbegotten wager blow up in his face?

Take nothing for granted. Never let your guard down.

"But don't worry, Rory will take care of your car while you're staying with us," Brodie said. "And I'll pay for the supplies as part of pay for helping with the kids and the house."

"Thank you," she said.

"You're welcome." His smile broadened to encompass his eyes.

"And thanks again for checking out my car, and I'm sorry I conked out on you last night." She reached out to touch his arm. Her fingers sizzled at the contact.

Brodie swallowed hard, and his Adam's apple bobbed. "Hey, feeding the hands was no problem. We used up the rest of the roast beef for sandwiches. Besides, you're doing me a big favor running after those two." Brodie jerked a thumb at the children.

Deannie peered over her shoulder. Buster was swinging on the horse's reins, and Angel was tugging at his bottom lip. Ranger tolerated their antics with long-suffering patience.

"Oh, heavens," Deannie exclaimed and hustled across the short distance to apprehend the two little scamps before they could dish out any more misery to the poor horse.

"Buster, let go of the reins. Angel, get your finger out of Ranger's mouth before he chomps it off."

Startled, Angel jerked her finger back and started to cry. Deannie squatted on the ground beside her and scooped the child into her lap. "What's wrong?"

"You ye'ded at me." Angel's bottom lip protruded.

"I'm sorry. I didn't mean to yell; I was just scared Ranger would bite you," Deannie apologized.

"Yeah, stoopid, whatcha mean sticking your finger in the horse's mouth?" her brother asked, placing his palms on his knees and wagging his head back and forth in front of Angel.

"I not stoopid," Angel declared, tears drying into salty streaks on her round cheeks. She jumped to her feet and knotted her tiny hands into fists. "I just wanted to see if he ated the sugar."

"Buster, it's not nice to call your sister names," Deannie said. "Tell her you're sorry."

Buster hung his head. "Sorry."

Deannie looked over at Brodie. He had a hand clamped over his mouth, and his shoulders shook with mirth.

"You're a big help."

"Hey, they're not my kids." He pursed his lips, still struggling to contain his laughter.

Why did the vivid image of a miniature Brodie and a small red-haired girl that looked just like her leap to mind? If she married this man, having his babies was a distinct possibility.

And having his children meant sex.

Deannie's heart thrilled at the idea of making love to Brodie. She envisioned his arms wrapped around her, those full lips giving her hot, wet kisses. She could almost taste him. Birth control would be in order. This sexy, virile man could get her pregnant simply by hanging his trousers next to hers.

Nervously, Deannie dropped her gaze; this was all too much to think about. Her plan had serious holes in it.

"Come on, Ranger, let's get you out of harm's way." Brodie chuckled and rescued his horse from Buster.

"Thanks again for checking out my car."

"It was all Rory."

"Yes, but it was on your dime."

His sharp eyes found her gaze, and she felt a sweet tickling low in her belly.

"Well, I best be getting back to work." He pulled the brim of his hat down lower over his dark eyes. "We usually eat supper at six-thirty. Will that be a problem?"

Deannie shook her head. "No problem."

No problem? Who was she kidding? She needed a crash course in cooking. The only thing she knew how to prepare was macaroni and cheese from a box.

Brodie swung astride his horse and gathered the reins in his hands. "See you then." Lifting his hand to his temple, he gave her a salute and trotted off across the pasture.

Deannie watched him go. He cut an impressive figure riding tall in the saddle, his broad shoulders swaying in practiced rhythm with his horse.

Something caught in Deannie's throat, an emotion

she couldn't name, and it fluttered there, unfettered by common sense.

Stop fantasizing about him, Deanna Hollis. There can't be a true romance between you two. Remember, no matter how attractive he might be, the man was still Rafe True-blood's son and her sworn enemy.

"MIX ONE-HALF CUP OF MILK WITH TWO CUPS OF breadcrumbs," Deannie read out loud from the recipe on the tablet screen in front of her. Biting her tongue in concentration, she followed the instructions.

Flour handprints graced the front of her apron. Her hair, which she'd pulled back into a ponytail, had worked itself loose, and strands of hair now trailed into her face. Deannie puffed out her cheeks and blew upward, trying to lift the escaping tendril out of her eyes, without having to use her hands.

Buster and Angel were being exceptionally cooperative, ensconced at the kitchen table where she'd left them with molding clay and cookie cutters.

Deannie poured the milk and breadcrumbs into the meat loaf and squished the mess with her hands. A memory stole over her. Here, in this very kitchen, she remembered her mother kneading bread on this same counter. She could hear her mom's melodious voice as she hummed "Down in the Valley."

For a fleeting moment, she saw her mother standing there, a welcome smile on her familiar face. Deannie's heart lurched. Her nose twitched. She knew it was all in her imagination, but a faint yeasty odor seemed to permeate the entire room.

"Oh, Mama," Deannie whispered under her breath, her chest tightening.

Any doubts she might harbor concerning her deception disappeared in that instant. Willow Creek belonged to her. The memories, so fresh and vivid, reassured her that this was her home. Her mother had lived here. Had died right out there in the horse paddock, thrown from an unruly stallion.

Deannie gulped against the tide of emotions running through her. They had cheated her of her birthright. Her past stolen, desecrated by those thieving Truebloods.

Except Brodie. He's different from Rafe and Kenny, the little voice in the back of her mind nudged.

She pushed that thought aside, clinging instead to her anger. Anger she'd cultivated for so many years. Anger intensified by her father's recent suicide.

Deannie clenched her fists, and ground meat oozed between her fingers. Somebody had to pay for what she'd suffered. Too bad it had to be Brodie.

Squaring her shoulders, Deannie mentally renewed her resolve. She had to win Brodie's heart, and she had to do it quickly.

"You not supposed to eat it." Buster's little voice snapped Deannie back to the moment. Uh-oh, this didn't sound good. What were those two up to?

"What are you kids doing?" she asked, standing on tiptoes to peer over the bar at the two imps at the table.

"She made a star," Buster explained. "But then she ate it."

"Angel!" Wiping her hands on her apron, Deannie darted around the corner to find Angel with a guilty expression and bits of blue clay sticking to her teeth.

"It didn't taste good." She made a face.

Deannie froze, her pulse racing. She had no idea what one should do in a situation like this. Call 9-1-1? Induce vomiting? Feed her bread?

She placed a palm under Angel's mouth. "Spit it out."

"Can't."

"Why not?"

"I swa'owed it."

Deannie groaned. She'd have to tell Brodie right away, but where was he? He could be anywhere on the ranch. Terrified, she wrung her hands and struggled to get control of her panic.

Think, Deannie, think.

The back door opened, and Brodie strolled inside.

"Thank God you're here!" Deannie breathed and rushed over to clutch his arm. It felt so strong and reassuring in her grasp that she had to choke back a lump of relief.

"They were that bad, huh?" Brodie's brown eyes crinkled at the edges, teasing her.

"No, Angel just ate some modeling clay; we've got to do something!" she said without taking a breath.

Brodie raised his palms. "Calm down, Deannie, you're talking a mile a minute, and I can't understand a word you're saying."

Buster and Angel hovered nearby, eyes wide in terror. Lord, she'd frightened them too.

"Angel poisoned herself with clay, and it's all my fault."

"Do you mean this?" Brodie strode across the room to retrieve the box of clay from the table. He held it up for her to see. In bright red letters, the box read "Non-Toxic."

"Oh."

Feeling like a monumental fool, Deannie dropped her gaze and studied the floor intently.

"Don't worry." Brodie chuckled, "Angel will be just fine."

"I'm sorry I panicked over nothing," Deannie apologized. "Trouble is, I'm not used to kids."

"Couldn't tell it by me," Brodie said, scooping Angel into his arms. "You're wonderful with them. And I'd rather have you worried unnecessarily than being lackadaisical like Matilda."

"I should have kept a closer eye on them," Deannie fretted. "But it was time to start supper, and I had to keep them occupied somehow. I never dreamed they'd *eat* the clay."

"*I* didn't eat it," Buster said, thrusting out his chest proudly.

"I sorry," Angel wailed. "I didn't mean to."

"Oh, sweetie." Deannie moved to where Brodie stood holding her and grasped Angel's little foot in her hand. "It's not your fault."

Brodie gave Deannie the once-over. She could just imagine how she appeared. Flour on her face, hair in disarray, apron askew. Flustered, Deannie pushed her hair from her face and retied her bedraggled apron strings.

"Looks like they've run you through the wringer," Brodie noted. "Tell you what, I'll take these two terrors off your hands while you finish fixing supper."

"Would you?"

She hadn't intended on sounding so desperate. She'd wanted to prove to Brodie that she could handle the children, cook dinner, and clean the house, but she'd failed miserably.

Without any wifely skills under her belt, how did she hope to coax him into marriage? He might find her attractive, yes, but she knew he would look for a wife who could help him run Willow Creek. With her current track record, she was lucky he hadn't asked her to pack her bags and get out like he had with Matilda.

"Unc' Brodie," Buster said, hopping from foot to foot. "I wanna piggyback ride."

"Hold on, partner. Let me bend down, and you crawl on."

"Yeah!" Buster said and placed a booted foot squarely in Brodie's back.

Brodie struggled to a standing position, Buster's arms wrapped tightly around his neck.

"You look like a packhorse." Deannie giggled.

"I feel like one."

"I don't know how single parents survive," she said. "Especially with more than one child."

"Neither do I." Brodie shook his head. "But I think sometimes a single-family household is better than a toxic home with two parents."

His eyes met Deannie's. His mouth drew down in a firm, hard line, and she wondered if he was thinking about Rafe. She knew what it was like to be disappointed with a father. She and Brodie had far more in common than Deannie cared to admit.

"I was about to go help Cooter feed the calves, you two want to come?" Brodie asked the kids.

"Yeah!" they hollered in unison.

Cooter? Cooter Gates?

Deannie's blood turned to ice at the mention of the foreman's name. When she'd started this charade, it had never occurred to her that Cooter Gates might still work at Willow Creek. Not after fifteen years. Not with the change in ownership.

What was she going to do? She'd only been seven years old when Cooter had last seen her, but how many red-haired Deannies had he met in the course of his lifetime? He was bound to put two and two together the minute he saw her and learned her name.

Fear swamped her. She'd couldn't fail. Not now. Not yet. Not without a fight. She'd waited too long for the day when she would be old enough, brave enough, and accomplished enough to get her home back.

Cooter had the power to send her scheme crashing down around her ears. One word from him and she would never have the chance to convince Brodie to fall in love with her, and she would never reclaim the family homestead. She had to avoid Cooter, that's all there was to it. But how?

"Deannie?"

She jerked her head up. Her pulse thudded furiously in the hollow of her neck.

"We'll be back in about an hour."

"Uh. Okay."

The screen door snapped shut behind them, the children's high-pitched giggles echoing in the distance.

Like a gambler holding a pair of deuces, whose bluff has been called, Deannie returned to the meat loaf with a heavy heart. Defeat was imminent unless she did something fast.

Throwing the meat loaf into the oven, she quickly peeled potatoes and set them on to boil. She opened a large can of green beans, dumped them into a pan, then slapped them on the stove to warm. Head down, hands clasped behind her back, she paced the tiled floor.

There's got to be a solution.

But instead of imagining a way out of her dilemma, she kept seeing Brodie's face. Cringing, she envisioned how he would look when Cooter recognized her and revealed who she really was. She saw Brodie's mouth harden into the same unforgiving expression he'd turned on Kenny the evening he found her playing cards at the Lonesome Dove.

Deannie shuddered. Her chance to live at Willow Creek Ranch again could forever shatter by one sentence from the old foreman.

Perhaps if she hid her hair. Tied it up in a scarf. It would buy her some time until she could come up with a permanent answer.

Grasping at straws, Deannie left the food cooking and scurried upstairs to her bedroom. She braided her hair and coiled it around her head. Pinning it into place, she covered the whole thing with a blue bandanna.

She looked at her reflection in the mirror and laughed. Well, if Brodie Trueblood was looking for a rancher's wife, he need search no farther. Staring back at her was the epitome of a country girl. Fresh-faced with no makeup, the apron stained with food, hair covered in a work scarf, sleeves rolled up for hard work, nobody would mistake her for a bar dolly now.

Please, let this work, she sent a prayer to the heavens, then hurried back downstairs just in time to finish cooking supper.

This was her plan. She'd set the table, lay out the food, then disappear upstairs when the ranch hands came stomping through the door. If Cooter caught sight of her, maybe he wouldn't think twice about her. She expected Brodie to check on her, but she had that covered. She'd tell him she had a headache.

Another fib.

Getting honorable now, Deannie? Her conscience gnawed. Dang. If Brodie had been like his father and brother, she would have no qualms about her scheme.

But he's not like them, is he?

No. He wasn't. Brodie was kind and generous, honest and true. But was she so wrong, hoping to marry him? After all, she was attracted to him and him to her, or so it seemed. What was so bad about marrying to get something? People did it all the time.

But not under false pretenses.

Deannie pressed her hands over her ears to drown out her nagging inner voice and didn't hear the footsteps on the back porch until it was too late to flee.

Trembling, she pressed her palms together and watched the back door swing open.

"Deannie?" Brodie. His boot heels scraped against the cement steps.

Her heart pounded in response. "Yes?" She twisted

her fingers into a knot behind her back and held her breath.

"Hi." He grinned, stepping into the room. "Something smells delicious."

"Where are the kids?" she asked. "I'll feed them in the kitchen."

"Rory's got them. They're right behind me." Brodie's eyes narrowed as he came closer. "Are you all right? You look funny."

"S-s-sure," she stammered. Heck, she didn't need Cooter to give her away; she was doing a damned fine job of it herself. "Why?"

"Your face is flushed. Like you have a fever."

Before she could react, he reached over and laid his palm across her forehead. That simple act sent blood surging through her veins in quick, vicious spurts. She felt lightheaded. Reaching out, she grasped the back of a chair and curled her fingers around it for support.

"Just hot in the kitchen."

"Is that why you tied your hair up?"

"Uh-huh." Why didn't he take his hand away!

"I guess that's it. You don't feel like you have a fever." Almost reluctantly, he dropped his arm to his side, and Deannie breathed a sigh of relief.

"I'm fine."

"That's good. I'd hate for you to get sick." His tenderness was a stake through her chest.

From outside she heard the others treading up the porch steps.

"Here come the troops," Brodie said. "You missed them at dinner yesterday, but now you'll meet everybody."

That's exactly what she was afraid of.

"Now that you mention it," Deannie said, fingering her brow, "I feel a sick headache coming on."

"I'll get you some aspirin," he offered.

But it was too late. The ranch hands poured through the door, Angel and Buster riding the shoulders of two men.

Deannie saw Cooter Gates, and she inhaled sharply, waiting for his cry of recognition.

The foreman ambled in, his hands moving before him to feel the way. Blinking, Deannie shook her head. She had recalled him as an old man, but that had been from a child's point of view. He was probably in his early sixties, she estimated, still slim, wearing the same western-style plaid shirts she remembered. His hair was grayer, and he sported a scraggly beard, but what captured her attention were his eyes.

Eyes that had once been blue and lively with a teasing light were now vacant and icy. Eyes ruined by too many days spent in the hot Texas sun without protective sunglasses. Eyes scarred white by cataracts.

One ranch hand offered his arm, and Cooter took it for support as he maneuvered into the dining room.

Realization struck Deannie hard. Sadness mingled with relief as she watched the older man settle into his chair.

Cooter was blind.

It saved her. Deannie took the old man's blindness as a clear, unmistakable sign. The heavens were in agreement. She was the rightful owner of Willow Creek Ranch.

7

W hat was the matter with Deannie? She was acting mighty skittish this evening. Was she still upset over Angel eating the clay?

Brodie slid a glance her way, but she hadn't spoken a word since supper. Those two preschoolers could definitely wear you out. Perhaps it was just a headache. But when he'd introduced her to Cooter, Deannie had gripped the table with both hands, and she'd held her breath for the longest time.

What was it Cooter had said? Something about having once known a little girl named Deannie. Why would that upset her?

Naw, he was reading more into things than was there.

Deannie washed dishes at the sink. She'd loaded the dishwasher, but with this crew, there were more dishes than there was room in the dishwasher. Metal utensils clanked against stainless steel. Her sleeves rolled up past her elbows, she seemed studiously intent on scrubbing the floral pattern off his mother's plates.

Thankfully, she had changed from that skimpy little halter top and those thigh-high denim shorts into jeans and a long-sleeved cotton shirt. The ranch hands were in the den watching television with Buster and Angel. Brodie finished clearing the table and brought the remaining dishes over to the sink.

His gaze trailed down Deannie's back and lingered on that well-toned tushy encased in those tight blue jeans. Brodie had a sudden urge to peel that bandana from her head, tug the pins from her hair, and let it float free and silky through his fingers.

"If you'll put Buster and Angel to bed, I'll finish the dishes," he offered.

Deannie turned to look at him. Her blue eyes, muted in the fluorescent lighting, appeared sad. "It's a deal."

"How's your headache?"

"It's gone."

"Maybe you'd like to come sit out on the porch with me when you get the kids down?"

"Maybe."

Her expression remained noncommittal, her tone even and devoid of emotion. He couldn't read her. What was she thinking?

"There's banana ice cream in the freezer. We could enjoy a bowl and watch the fireflies flicker through the honeysuckle," he tempted.

"Maybe."

She took the children upstairs, and Brodie turned his attention to the dishes. It was nice having Deannie around the house, he admitted. All day he'd looked forward to coming home and getting to know her better.

He prayed Buster and Angel would be so tired they'd fall asleep as soon as their heads hit their pillows. He wanted Deannie with him on the front porch swing, looking up at the stars and telling him all about herself.

The television clicked off, and the ranch hands shuffled through the kitchen, Rory guiding Cooter around the furniture. They wished Brodie goodnight and soon disappeared out the back door.

Thankful silence ensued.

Brodie wiped down the countertop, then checked his watch. Feeling more nervous than Rafe at an old-fashioned tent revival prayer meeting, Brodie paced the kitchen. It wasn't good to be so anxious. This inexplicable magnetism drawing Brodie to her could lead him into trouble if he wasn't careful.

The stairs creaked, and his pulse skipped. Swallowing hard, Brodie retrieved the ice cream from the freezer in the corner and scooped some into two bowls. Without looking up, he heard her enter the kitchen on kitten-quiet feet.

"Kids down for the count?" He smiled.

Deannie nodded. "It only took four pages of *Curious George*."

"They had fun today," Brodie commented. "I haven't seen them laugh this much since Emma left Kenny. It's been tough on them."

"Family problems usually are."

Something flickered in her eyes. Something dark.

Something hidden deep inside her. Was she speaking from personal experience?

"The children like you," Brodie said, handing Deannie a bowl of ice cream.

She'd taken her hair down, he noticed, his body instantly responding to the lovely sight. Turning, he stowed the ice cream carton back in the freezer. "When I took them outside to feed the calves, they chattered about you nonstop."

"I like them, too." A soft smile lifted her mouth. "It's funny. I've never been around small children, and I thought I wouldn't enjoy it much, but I do."

"They can be a handful, no doubt about it." Brodie placed his hand lightly on Deannie's elbow. "But they are great."

To his delight, she didn't pull back. Instead, she allowed him to guide her down the hallway and out onto the front porch.

"We'll leave the door open," he said. "In case the kids wake up and call for us."

"You act like their father."

Brodie frowned. "That's because their own father won't assume his responsibilities." Thinking of his brother sent a spark of anger flaring through him. "But let's not ruin the moment by talking about Kenny. I just want to sit here with you and enjoy my ice cream."

The porch swing chains creaked as they settled into it together. The dish of ice cream burned cold in his hands.

A slight breeze blew, tousling Deannie's flame-red mane. Cicadas buzzed in the mimosa tree on the front lawn. Buster's tricycle sat overturned on the sidewalk. The large climbing yellow rosebush his mother had planted fifteen years ago was in full bloom, crawling all over the white lattice trellis. The sweet aroma drifted over to them.

Brodie remembered when they had planted that bush. He and Mama together. His mother had been so proud to finally have a permanent place to call her own. And not just a humble home but a fine farmhouse. Overnight, she'd gone from a shanty to Willow Creek Ranch.

He knew his mother had always felt guilty about the way Rafe got the ranch, but she'd been so excited over their own good fortune, she had pushed thoughts of that other family aside. She'd stuck by her husband through the bad times, and Melinda Trueblood considered the ranch her reward for putting up with so much.

Looking out across the yard, Brodie wondered what had happened to Gil Hollis and his little daughter. She'd be grown by now, he realized. In her early twenties. Now with Rafe gone, maybe he could track her down, find some way to make amends for what had happened. He imagined she held no love for Truebloods.

Shaking his head to dispel Gil Hollis, Brodie turned his attention to the woman at his side.

Deannie, too, surveyed the surrounding land. She sat up straight, her posture rigid, a faraway expression in her eyes as if she were viewing something from the past. Once again, he got the strangest sensation she was hiding something.

"You've got a beautiful place here, Brodie."

"Thank you. It is my pride and joy. When my father...er...bought it..." He hesitated over the words.

BRODIE

No point telling Deannie the sordid truth about his old man. At least not yet. "The previous owner had a drinking problem and had allowed the place to fall into ruins."

"And your *father* fixed it up."

Was that sarcasm in her voice? Startled, Brodie studied her face. Had she heard about Rafe? What had Kenny divulged during that card game?

"No," Brodie said. "I'm the one who made Willow Creek into the thriving spread it is today."

"You must be very proud." More sarcasm? Her face was neutral.

"I've worked hard for everything I've achieved."

"I'll bet."

He stared at her. There was definitely an undercurrent.

"Your ice cream is melting." She pointed at his bowl and peeked over at him.

He could smell her sweet magnolia scent. Her aroma mingled with the taste of ice cream, and he was charmed. "My father died a little over two weeks ago," Brodie said. "I guess I haven't really come to grips with his death."

She clicked her tongue. "I know how hard it is."

"My father and I weren't very close. But oddly, that makes it harder to accept. Now I'll never be able to tell him that I did love him despite everything that happened between us."

"That's a shame."

"What about your father?" he asked.

"My father's dead, too. He passed away six months

81

ago, and we were very close." She stirred her spoon in the melted ice cream.

"So you understand."

"Yes."

"You feel unsettled, disjointed, out of place. Like nothing that seemed important before matters anymore. You start looking for answers to impossible questions, like 'what's the meaning of life?' and 'why am I here?' It's distressing."

"Exactly." Deannie shrugged. "That's the reason I was headed for New Mexico. I'm looking for a fresh start. There's nothing to keep me in Texas."

"Nothing?"

She shook her head.

"Hmm."

"Hmm?" She grinned. "What does that mean?"

"Actually," he said, "I wanted to talk to you about your trip to New Mexico."

"Oh?" She studied him with her steady gaze.

Suddenly the air left Brodie's body as surely as if he had been thrown from the back of his horse. Why did a single glance from this woman knock his emotions every which way?

"Yeah," he said once he'd inhaled again. "I've been thinking, even after Emma gets back home, we will still need someone around to do the cooking and cleaning."

"What are you saying?" Deannie pursed those peachy lips, and Brodie just about choked on his ice cream.

"I'm offering you the housekeeper job permanently. That is if you're interested."

She didn't answer right away.

"It pays two thousand a month plus room and board. I know it's not a fortune, but we sure could use the help." Lord, why did he want so badly for her to say yes?

"I must think about it."

"Do you have someone special waiting for you in Santa Fe?"

Damn! Why had he asked that question? Brodie set his empty bowl down on the porch and avoided her gaze. He waited, breath bated, for her response.

"No one."

"So, no family there?"

"I have no family left. I was looking for a new start."

Stay here. Start here. His heart tripped. "Uh...I've got another reason for hoping you'll take this job."

"What's that?" One auburn eyebrow arched prettily.

Brodie shifted and moved closer to her. He rested his arm on the back of the swing. His boots scraped against the porch, and the swing's chain squeaked its protest.

"I like you, Deannie." His voice was gruffer than he intended, smoky from the heated emotions burning his chest.

"I like you too, Brodie." Her smile was genuine, honest, and filled him to the bursting point.

"But all legitimate." He hastened to add, fearful that she might read an ulterior motive into his job offer. He didn't want her believing he was conspiring to take advantage of her. "This is strictly a business arrangement. I want you to know that I don't have hanky-panky on my mind."

"You don't?" Her tone was rich, cool as silk.

"No, ma'am." He ran a hand through his hair, feeling naked without his cowboy hat.

"Why not?"

Her question surprised him so much that Brodie almost toppled off the porch swing. Here's where he needed to tiptoe. Before he got more deeply involved with her, he needed to discover whether she was interested in Brodie, the person, or the successful rancher.

"Because I respect you."

She eyed him. "You're not pulling my leg, are you?"

"Absolutely not."

Tilting her head, her eyes narrowed. "You're a breed all your own, Brodie Trueblood."

"I'm probably not like the men you're used to."

"No," she said, "you're not. But I'm glad for that."

It was time to tell her what was on his mind. Brodie didn't believe in playing mind games or toying with someone's affections.

"Truth is, Deannie, I want to get to know you better, but I need to take things slowly. There's a lot going on in my life—settling my father's estate, getting used to having Emma and her three kids living in the house, dealing with my brother, Kenny, keeping the ranch on track. I have little time for dating, but I will eventually. How do you feel about that?"

"Let me see if I understand you correctly." Deannie tucked a strand of hair behind her ear. "You're seeking a professional relationship between us, but you think you might be open to changing that relationship in the future?"

Her eyes glistened in the moonlight, and in that instant, Brodie felt as if he could see right into her soul.

Her pupils widened, and an odd sensation grabbed him with an urgency he didn't understand. This emotional thread between them seemed to transcend time and place. To carry them beyond the mundane and up into the stars.

He'd never been one to believe in reincarnation and past lives and all that other New Age stuff, but if such things were true, Brodie would swear he'd known Deannie in another existence. The invisible cord binding them was that startling, that strong.

"Yes," he mumbled, barely able to speak.

"Before I accept your offer, there's one thing I need to know."

"What's that?"

"Under your arrangement, does this mean you couldn't kiss me?"

Warning, danger, proceed at your own risk! Be careful, Trueblood.

"Do you *want* me to kiss you?"

In answer, she allowed her eyes to drift closed and tilted her chin up.

Should he kiss her? Was it smart?

Brodie clenched his jaw, his mind at war with his body. He wanted to taste her so badly it caused a searing ache deep down in his soul.

"Brodie," she cooed, soft as the evening breeze raising the hairs on his wrists.

Stifling a groan, he succumbed to temptation and closed the small gap between them. The swing rocked back and forth as he gathered her into his arms.

He rested his cheek against the top of her head. Her hair smelled of magnolia flowers and warm sunshine. He felt her heart beating against her slender rib cage, tapping out a frantic flurry. She wanted him. Whether the desire was purely physical or something more, he couldn't tell, but he could tell she was not faking her response.

Her entire body trembled. Her back arched, and she pushed her chest hungrily against his. Tossing her head, she whimpered and exposed her long neck.

Brodie took the invitation for what it was and lowered his mouth to cover an enticing patch of her peaches-and-cream complexion.

Deannie melted at his touch, going limp in his arms as his tongue explored her vulnerable throat.

Like an out-of-control brushfire, sexual need leaped through him, chaotic and desperate. It had been years since he'd been with a woman and never with one who turned him on as much as Deannie.

He knew he should put an end to this before it got out of control, but he couldn't. Not yet. Not without a taste of those beguiling lips.

Brodie wanted her. Here. Now. This minute and no amount of self-coaxing and cajoling could stop him.

"Deannie," he whispered and took her mouth.

Their kiss flared like a match touched to gasoline. She was the candle, and he the wick.

His forcefulness did not frighten her. She drank him in, her lips soft, cool, and tasting of banana ice cream.

Her teeth parted, allowing him entry.

Brodie's tongue darted inside the moist recesses of her mouth, and a thrill shot clean through his bones. He felt free, unrestrained, wild. It was an incredible sensation, similar to busting an unruly stallion.

For too long, he'd kept a damper on his emotions, tamping down his feelings to stay even-keeled. Biting his tongue when he longed to tell his father what he thought of him and his itinerant lifestyle. Such restraint had led him to hold back in other areas of his life.

Like in romance.

In reality, he'd always been a little afraid of losing himself in a relationship. He'd seen firsthand what blind love had done to his mother and Emma. They'd both loved Trueblood men, and it earned them nothing but heartache. Although he longed for a woman to offer him that kind of devotion, it also terrified him—she was a woman who liked to party and gamble and hang out in bars.

A woman like Deannie.

That sobering thought splashed over him, ice-water cold and just as startling. It was true, he'd first met her in a bar, drinking and playing cards with Kenny and his friends. And now she was here, kissing him, a virtual stranger, with untamed abandon.

But what about the sweet woman who had cared so tenderly for Angel and Buster, the hopeful voice in the back of his head urged. Would someone out for a good time take on those kids? Was he making value judgments on her based on his family history and not seeing her clearly for who she was?

Just because a woman liked to have fun didn't mean she was trouble. Maybe it was time to check some of his prejudices and old-fashioned values at the door and reevaluate his outlook before it stunted him.

"Brodie?"

He blinked, realizing he had stopped kissing her and pulled away.

"What's wrong?" She sat up and touched his shoulder.

Brodie suppressed a quiver and closed his eyes briefly, trying hard to regain control of himself. "I'm sorry," he said. "I didn't mean for things to go so far."

"You just kissed me. That's all."

"Openmouthed."

"Is that too friendly?"

"For a first kiss? Yeah, maybe."

She fingered her lips, self-doubt written on her face. He hated that he'd caused her to doubt herself.

"It's not you," he explained. "I locked up my heart a long time ago, and well...relationships don't come easily to me."

"Me either."

He studied her face. "I've been in an emotional deep freeze, but when I'm around you, I feel myself starting to thaw. It's scary." *But good.*

"Does the job offer still stand?"

He avoided looking at her. One glance into those her eyes and he'd be lost again. "Yeah," he said. "But I think we'd better forgo the kissing for a while. Like I said, I want to get to know you better first, and kissing complicates things."

She nodded, offering a faint smile. "I agree."

Brodie got to his feet and walked to the edge of the porch. *Take a deep breath, Trueblood, and cool down.* He sucked in the sweet spring air, slipped his hands into his back pockets, and stared out across the land.

The land that meant so much to him. The land he'd

pampered and cultivated into the thriving outfit it was today. The land that suddenly seemed empty and worthless without someone to share the future with.

Could Deannie be that someone? *Whoa, getting way ahead of yourself, partner.*

"Brodie?"

The porch swing creaked, and he felt her come up behind him. He half turned and peered at her over his shoulder.

"I think we can make this work. I'm very much attracted to you, but I'm also leery of getting involved too quickly. I've been hurt in the past, and I want to take things as slowly as you do."

"Yeah?" he asked, his tone low and throaty even to his own ears.

"I'm saying it would be an honor to accept the position as your housekeeper. But let's put a time limit on it."

"For how long?"

"Let's say for the next three months, we keep our relationship strictly professional, if at the end of that time, if we're both still interested, we consider exploring something more personal. Is it a deal?" Deannie thrust her small hand toward him, an intense expression on her face.

"Deal." They shook on it.

She was murmuring all the right words, stoking the heat under his hopes and dreams. He had to be very careful because Brodie knew one thing for sure. Deannie had his heartstrings clutched firmly in a downward tug, and she was yanking with all her might.

❧ 8 ❧

Brodie had played right into her plans.

She knew he'd been aching to get close to her. She'd seen desire masked in his dark eyes, read the intense longing in his body language. After that earth-shattering kiss, when it seemed he might fold his hand in fear and retract the job offer, she'd quickly backed off, letting him think she wanted to take things as slowly as he did.

Too bad the man didn't play poker; she could win back Willow Creek from him in one game. Deannie slid her eyes up and down Brodie's lean, muscular body.

Now, if the man played strip poker that would be a whole other story.

The image of enacting strip poker with this ruggedly handsome man sent a heated flush rushing up her neck.

Deannie took her palm, the one that Brodie had just shaken, the one that still burned from his touch, and pressed it against her thigh. She wanted him to offer marriage, yes. Her sole intent was to win Willow Creek, whatever the cost. But she couldn't lose her head. For no matter how different he seemed on the surface, Brodie was still Rafe Trueblood's son, and the acorn didn't fall far from the tree.

Trouble was, Brodie's kiss had stirred her own desires. Desires she'd suppressed in favor of revenge. Desires she'd denied, had never investigated, for fear she would lose her drive to regain the ranch. Suddenly, she faced corralling intense longings, and she wasn't sure how to go about it.

This is stupid, Deannie. If your plan will work, you can't allow your feelings to get out of control. Remember, no matter how attractive he is, Brodie's a Trueblood and no friend of yours.

Recalling what Brodie had said earlier about Gil Hollis not living up to his responsibilities and letting Willow Creek fall to ruin aroused Deannie's anger and cooled her ardor.

Brodie had lied, telling her Rafe had purchased the ranch, when in reality his old man had stolen the property from her father.

High-beam headlights shone down the gravel road in front of the house as a vehicle rounded the corner.

"Looks like we got company," Brodie said.

A pickup truck with a loud muffler chugged into the drive. Brodie's face dissolved into a frown.

"Who is it?" she asked.

"Kenny." Brodie snorted.

A sudden knot of fear twisted Deannie's stomach. How much had she revealed to Kenny during their card game? Would he tell Brodie she'd tried to get him to wager the ranch?

The truck door slammed, echoing loudly into the night. Kenny weaved a path over to the front porch. "Hey, li'l brother."

"What are you doing here?"

"I come to see my kids."

"They're in bed." Brodie folded his arms across his chest and widened his stance.

"Wake 'em up."

"No."

Kenny doubled up his fists. "Wake them up."

"I will not fight you."

"Chicken. The old man was right; you're nothing but a coward."

Standing behind him like she was, Deannie could almost feel Brodie's anger. He clenched his hands and inhaled sharply. She could tell the old hurt that ran deep between the two brothers was nothing new. Deannie understood Brodie's conflict with his older brother. Her own father had disappointed her in countless ways. Chief among them, losing Willow Creek Ranch.

"Go home," Brodie said.

"I come to see my kids, dammit."

"You can see them tomorrow."

"Get out of my way." Swinging his arms, Kenny started up the porch.

Brodie moved to block him. "It's ten o'clock. They've been in bed for over an hour."

Kenny looked surprised as if he did not understand time. "I'll wake them up if you won't."

"You will not. You're thinking of what you want, not what those babies need."

"Like what?"

"You reek of whiskey. You remind me so much of Rafe it's sickening."

"Don't you talk to me like that, you little snot." Kenny ducked his head and charged Brodie.

Deannie squealed and slapped a hand over her mouth. She'd witnessed more than her share of these kinds of altercations, and they only ended one way—somebody gets beat up. But it would be to her advantage if the two brothers stayed mad at each other. A fight would cement their differences of opinion and keep Kenny from blabbing to Brodie about that card game at the Lonesome Dove.

Brodie sidestepped, and Kenny crashed into the porch swing.

Bellowing like a bull charging a matador, Kenny turned and dove at Brodie again. Calmly, Brodie wadded up his fist and punched Kenny squarely on the jaw.

Crumpling like cellophane, Kenny sank to the porch.

"I've never seen you this bad off, big brother. What's happened to you?" Brodie asked, squatting beside Kenny.

Despite the harshness in his voice, Deannie could tell Brodie still loved his brother. Just as she had loved her father despite all of his failings. How different things would have been if her mother hadn't died. Daddy probably wouldn't have turned to alcohol to soothe his emotional pain, and he would never have lost Willow Creek. She would have been raised by her adoring parents and supportive community. She would have been invited to the prom and gone to college.

Instead, she'd spent most of her childhood in shacks

and bars. She'd suffered cruel taunts at school and endured her father's drinking binges. She'd never had a boyfriend, nor even many friends. Her education had come from the school of hard knocks. Learning to play poker to win back Willow Creek had become all-consuming.

Deannie stood in the shadows, watching the drama between the two brothers unfold. Even though she was an outsider, she had a vested interest in the outcome. If the Trueblood men made peace with each other, she stood a good chance of having Kenny expose her as a conniving

schemer just when she was getting Brodie on her side.

"What in the hell is wrong with you?" Brodie asked his brother.

"Emma," Kenny said with a strangled cry. Grunting, he maneuvered himself into a sitting position. "I went to see her at the hospital. Emma told me she wants a divorce."

"Can you blame her?"

"When she walked out on me two weeks ago, I thought this would blow over. That being nine months pregnant and hormonal had put her in a snit. Especially when she came to stay with you. I asked myself how mad could she be if she chose Willow Creek instead of going to her parents in Midland."

"You've pushed her to the limit."

Maudlin tears misted Kenny's eyes. "She looked so pretty sitting up in the hospital bed wearing that pink housecoat I bought her when she had Angel. Emma's always looked gorgeous in pink. She was nursing the baby when I came in, but she wouldn't even look at me."

"You've put her through a lot, Kenny. A woman can only take so much." Brodie extended his hand and tugged his brother to his feet.

"Mama never divorced the old man."

"Is that your excuse? The old man acted like a creep, and Mama kept taking it, so you thought you'd try it on Emma?"

Kenny's bottom lip trembled. "I love her, Brodie."

"You got a damned funny way of showing it."

"Well, everyone can't be Mr. Holier-Than-Thou like you," Kenny snarled. "This is all your fault."

"How do you figure that?" Brodie sank his hands on his hips and glared at his older brother.

Deannie stepped away and pressed her back against the cool wood of the farmhouse. Neither of them seemed to notice her. She understood their pain, but she did not want to empathize with the Truebloods. She couldn't afford to care about them. She had to feed her anger to do what she had to do.

"If Rafe hadn't deeded you the ranch in his will, Emma would never have left me," Kenny mumbled.

"I didn't ask Rafe to leave the whole thing to me. I was as surprised by the inheritance as you. In fact, it would have been just like him to shut me out completely."

"That's not true. The old man was damned proud of what you did with this ranch. Why else do you think he left it to you? He knew I'd lose it the same way he stole it."

Brodie snorted and turned his head. The look on his face told her he was fighting some intense emotions.

"I'm a screw-up," Kenny said glumly. "I've lost the best thing I've ever had." Tears slipped down his face.

Moving across the porch to cover the short distance between them, Brodie laid a comforting arm across Kenny's shoulder. "I can help you," he said. "Dammit, Kenny, I *want* to help you. I'd hate to see you drink yourself to death at fifty-five the way the old man did."

Kenny clung to his brother. "Would you do that for me?"

"You bet. But you've got to do exactly as I say."

"I'll try," Kenny said, clasping the hand Brodie extended. "What do I have to do?"

"First, you've got to quit drinking."

Kenny nodded. "I'll give it my best shot."

"No," Brodie said, "your best shot won't do. You've *got* to stop."

Rubbing his bleary eyes, Kenny considered his brother's words. "All right."

"Second, move in here where I can keep an eye on you."

"I can't move in here," Kenny protested. "Emma's staying here when she gets released from the hospital. She'll leave if I stay."

"Emma won't have to know you're here. Not until you've had time to get your act together and find a job. Tonight, you can sleep in the bunkhouse with the hands. Tomorrow, we'll clean up the cabin on the back forty and you can move in."

Papaw's cabin. Deannie had forgotten about the old place. It was the first house her great-grandfather built at Willow Creek in 1925. A tiny one-room cabin constructed for him and his new bride.

"Deannie will see to it you get your meals." Brodie jerked his thumb in her direction. "I just hired her as our new housekeeper."

Kenny swung his gaze in her direction, surprise on his face as if noticing her standing in the shadows for the first time. "Hey," he said, pointing a finger. "You're the one who wiped me out of seven hundred dollars."

9

Looking hangdog, Kenny went back to his truck, and drove to the bunkhouse.

Hands clasped behind her back, Deannie eased toward the door. She wanted to get away from Brodie as quickly as possible before he quizzed her about what Kenny had said.

"Wait. I want to speak with you." Brodie's voice halted her.

"Can't this wait until morning?" She faked a yawn. "I'm exhausted."

"No, it can't. I've got to close up the barn. Please wait for me in the kitchen."

"Okay." Deannie gulped, a thousand fearful thoughts racing through her mind. At least he hadn't told her to pack her bags. Not yet, anyway.

She waited in the darkened kitchen, her arms crossed over her chest. Moonlight spilled in through the open window, and the breeze stirred the curtains. The clock on the wall chimed eleven. Her moment of truth had arrived.

Ask not for whom the bell tolls.

The floorboards creaked, riveting Deannie's attention to the doorway. Brodie stepped into the room, his face cloaked in shadows. He flicked on the light switch, and Deannie blinked against the glare that shone brighter than an interrogator's lamp.

Her pulse thumped.

"Who are you?" Brodie demanded.

"Wh-what do you mean? I'm Deannie McCellan," she said. Did he suspect she was actually Deanna Hollis? Was her game over before it started? Deannie gulped, terrified that she was about to be unceremoniously kicked off the grounds of Willow Creek.

"You're a professional gambler, aren't you?" Brodie's tone was icy. He pushed his fingers through his hair and sighed. "That's why you were in the Lonesome Dove last night. You were hustling poker."

Deannie opened her mouth. This might be the time to come clean. To at least admit to some truth. "I'm not a professional gambler."

"If you can take my brother for that amount of money, then you've got to be damned good."

"I'm not too bad."

"You lied to me. You told me you were so broke you couldn't afford to have your car repaired."

"I didn't lie. I am broke."

"What did you do with Kenny's money?"

"I gave it to charity."

Brodie glared at her. "I don't believe you."

"It's the truth."

"Give me one good reason to buy that story."

Deannie stared at her feet. She couldn't tell him why she'd given her ill-gotten winnings to July Haynes at the homeless shelter.

"There's not a job waiting for you in Santa Fe, is there? You made that up, too."

Miserably, she shook her head.

"You seem pretty adept at lying and gambling. I can tell you've spent your fair share of time in bars." He grasped the back of a chair with both hands. "I've got to say, Deannie, that concerns me."

How much could she tell Brodie without giving herself away? She had to say something, or he would show her the door.

"I learned to play poker from watching my father," she said. "He had a gambling problem. Drinking problem, too."

"So, you've followed in his footsteps."

"*No.*" She hated for him to believe that of her.

Arching an eyebrow, he waited for her to continue. Skeptical, but giving her a chance at least.

"I drink hardly at all, and I don't have a gambling problem. Sometimes when I run low on cash, I get into a poker game, but that's it. I know what you're thinking, Brodie, and you're wrong. I don't have a problem."

"You know," Brodie said, "I should probably fire you."

She raised a trembling hand to her mouth. "What's that?"

"My father was a professional gambler. I saw first-hand what he did to himself and the people that loved him. He denied he had a problem. He refused to reform. That's why I'm willing to help Kenny. He really wants a better life. And that's why I'm willing to give you a chance too."

"Brodie..."

"I will insist on one thing."

"What's that?"

"I won't tolerate lies. From now on, be honest with me."

"All right," she promised, even knowing that she was headed for one hell of a fall.

❦

BRODIE DIDN'T KNOW WHETHER TO BELIEVE HIS HEAD or his heart. His head urged him to forget Deannie, to run as fast as he could in the opposite direction, but his heart cried out for him to accept her at face value.

Feeling oddly untethered, he sat at the kitchen table, his hands clasped together in front of him. From the moment his family moved in at Willow Creek Ranch, the kitchen had been his favorite room. His mother loved to cook, and that's how he remembered her best, standing at the oven creating delicious dishes for her family.

Taking a deep breath, Brodie closed his eyes. He could almost smell her fresh-baked apple pies cooling on the sideboard. If he lingered long enough in the memory, his tongue would tingle with the taste of cinnamon, sugar, and flaky crust.

Melinda Trueblood made this house a real home for him and Kenny. She'd sewn curtains for the windows and stenciled the walls with a floral design. She'd cut fresh flowers from the garden and placed them in vases around the house. She set the table with dishes from Dollar General, the best she could afford, and scheduled the supper for six-thirty, hoping to create a normal family routine.

But Rafe had never cooperated, and Kenny was soon following after him, disappearing for days at a time, returning with smug grins and no explanations for their behavior. Mostly it had been Brodie and his mother dining alone at the big table built for twelve.

Sorrow pushed at the back of his eyelids. Brodie swallowed hard and choked off the emotions. There was nothing he could do about the past. He couldn't resurrect his mother, nor could he save his father. The most he could do was make sure he lived a decent, moral life.

And the only way to ensure that was to avoid women who'd spent their time in bars playing poker.

You shouldn't judge her. You don't even know her. He heard his mother's kind, forgiving voice in his head and immediately felt guilty for making assumptions. *Give her a chance.*

Brodie opened his eyes and cradled his head in his hands. He was bone-weary, but sleep evaded him. Why was he so attracted to the one person who could cause him the most grief?

DEANNIE GAVE AN UNLADYLIKE SNORT AND FLOPPED over onto her side. She punched her pillow for good measure. Who was Brodie Trueblood to pass judgment on her life? He didn't even know who she really was.

Calm down, Deannie, getting mad won't solve anything.

With the current turn of events, Deannie sorely regretted playing poker with Kenny. It had set her back in her goal of winning Brodie's heart. Had she known that Rafe would die so young, Deannie wouldn't have wasted her time training to be an ace poker player. If she'd known Brodie would be so damned good-looking, that he loathed gambling and that he'd inherited Willow Creek instead of Kenny, she would have set her cap for him from the beginning.

But the past was past. She had no choice but to deal the hand fate dealt her.

The worst thing she could do at this point was crowd Brodie. She had one option—assume her house-keeping duties, stay on her best behavior, and avoid being alone with Brodie. But just because she had to maintain a professional relationship with the man, it didn't mean she couldn't use every other seductive tool in her arsenal.

Deannie smiled in the darkness.

She would cook the best meals he'd ever tasted. She'd care for Buster and Angel as if they were her own kids. When Emma came home from the hospital, she would befriend the woman and become indispensable to her as well. She would clean, she would sew, and she would do her best to prove to Brodie that she could be the rancher's perfect wife.

Then it would only be a matter of time before Brodie longed for the other things a wife could offer. By then, she'd have him hook, line, and sinker, and she would take her rightful place as mistress of Willow Creek Ranch.

Deannie shivered at the memory of his kisses and hugged herself.

Come on, Deannie, you've got to stay in control. How can you hope to manipulate Brodie into marriage if you don't stay in control?

Manipulate. Such an ugly word. But that was exactly what she was doing.

As if Rafe Trueblood hadn't manipulated your father.

Daddy had been vulnerable after Mama's death, and Rafe preyed upon his weakness.

Brodie isn't his father.

Maybe not, but he was the owner of her home. Deannie fisted her hands as the old memories swept through her. Memories that fueled her need for revenge. Memories powerful enough to throttle her guilt.

She remembered that long-ago night as vividly as if fifteen minutes had passed instead of fifteen years. Bile rose in Deannie's throat, hot and acidic. She had been sleeping in the room down the hall from this one. The room where Buster and Angel now slept.

Back then that room had been decorated in shades of pink, from dusty rose to cotton candy to bubble gum. She had a canopy bed with a dainty pink coverlet and lace curtains to match. She recalled the rocking chair Daddy had carved by hand, a massive doll collection including twenty-two Barbies and tons of accessories.

A little girl's dream.

A dream that had shattered into a nightmare when her daddy had come stumbling into her bedroom, tears streaming down his face.

"Deannie, honey, wake up," he'd said.

Since Mama's death six months earlier, life had become unstable and insecure. Daddy, who used to rise early in the morning and work the ranch by dawn, now lay in bed until noon. Often, he would forget to eat or even take a shower. He stopped taking Deannie to church and refused to see friends when they tried to visit.

He'd once been a cheerful man who whistled and sang. Now he frowned frequently and rarely spoke. He began selling off the cattle to pay his gambling debts, and he let most of the ranch help go.

Deannie saw her father less and less. He left her in the care of a housekeeper, occasionally for days at a time.

Back then she hadn't really understood what was going on. It was only later she came to realize he'd been gambling and drinking those nights when he disappeared into Rascal.

"Deannie." Her father had shaken her and turned on the bedside lamp. The muted light sent shadows jumping across the room. "Come on now, wake up."

Clutching her teddy bear to her chest, her heart pounding, Deannie had scooted up in the bed. Rubbing the sleep from her eyes, she'd stared at the man who'd become a stranger to her. Fear, very similar to what she'd felt when her mother had been killed, clamped a cold hand over her trembling body. Something awful had happened. She knew it.

"Daddy! What's wrong?"

He looked terrible. His eyes were bleary and bloodshot, his clothes rumpled. His hair was in disarray, and he smelled funny. Deannie remembered crinkling her nose in distaste, torn between the desire to hug her father and the repulsion over his stench.

"Get up. Get dressed."

"Why, Daddy? Did someone die?"

"No." Her father threw back the covers. "Get up, Deannie, right this minute."

"Are we going somewhere?" That thought had cheered her temporarily. It would be nice to go on a trip, just her and Daddy.

"Yeah." He'd nodded grimly. "We're going somewhere."

"Where?" Her fear had momentarily slipped away. "To the beach?"

"No."

"Disneyland?"

"No." He got on his hands and knees and lifted the dust ruffle on her bed as he searched beneath it. Deannie remembered peering down at him from the bed and noticing the bald spot on the top of his head she'd never remembered seeing before. He pulled out her pink suitcase. It was covered with dust. "Pack your favorite clothes and toys."

His harsh tone brought the fear rippling back.

"Daddy," she'd whispered, curling a hand to her mouth. "You're scaring me."

That's when she'd heard a noise at her bedroom door. Boots scraping the hardwood floor, spurs jangling.

The memory slowed and narrowed in focus. Deannie's throat constricted at the old vision so vivid in her mind. A scene as sharp and clear at this moment as it had been the night it played out.

Deannie wadded her pillow in her fists, closed her eyes, and tried unsuccessfully to block the memory.

She'd swiveled her head to the doorway. Recalled the stark terror that had driven through her small body at what she'd seen standing there.

A man. Tall, thin, dressed completely in black. He sported a narrow mustache, numerous tattoos, diamond rings on his pinkie fingers, and a wide, gold belt buckle.

Even now, Deannie's blood ran cold, and the hair on her forearms raised.

He looked exactly like a silent-movie villain with his dark hair slicked back off his forehead, his thin lips curled smugly at the corners, and his hips cocked in an insouciant pose.

For the first and last time, Deanna Rene Hollis clapped eyes on the man who would forever change her life. The slick man who'd snatched away her innocence, leaving her bitter and vengeful. The man who'd instilled a hatred inside her so savage it would last fifteen years and spill out onto his sons.

Rafe Trueblood.

He had cocked his head to one side and winked at her. Then he'd pulled a cigar from his front shirt pocket. Striking a match with his thumbnail, he'd lit his cigar and watched her father as he scurried around the room, opening drawers and pulling stuff from the closet.

"Don't get hysterical, Hollis. I told you there was no need for you and your girl to leave tonight. Tomorrow will suit me just fine."

"Daddy?" Her voice had risen high and shrill, more of a demand than a question.

"Hush, Deannie, and get dressed."

"No reason to pull the girl from her bed at midnight."

"Yes, there is. Willow Creek doesn't belong to us anymore."

"You're losing it, Hollis. I don't want it being said around Rascal I kicked a child out in the middle of the night."

"Perhaps you should have thought about that before you cheated me out of my homestead." Daddy was panting.

Rafe walked across the floor, blowing smoke rings. He thrust his face into Daddy's. "I don't cheat. You stink at poker. It's not my fault you can't hold your liquor and you let your mouth overload your butt."

Deannie coughed and curled her knees up under her chin, frozen, welded to her bed, staring at the two men arguing in front of her.

"Did you hear me, Deannie?" her father snarled, spinning away from Rafe and turning to glare at her. "Out of the bed, now!"

"Please, Daddy," she begged, hot tears running down her cheeks. "Tell me why."

Rafe held up a palm. "Please allow me to field this question for you, Hollis."

Her daddy clenched his hands so tight that his knuckles turned white.

Smiling, Trueblood stepped toward the bed. "Your daddy bet this ranch and all the contents on a hand of poker. Do you know what that means?"

Deannie shook her head. Rafe Trueblood's breath was warm and smelled worse than her daddy's body odor.

"It means he lost the card game, and now Willow Creek Ranch belongs to me."

Deannie's bottom lip trembled. "I don't live here anymore? What about my toys and my clothes?"

"I'm sorry, darling, but you're gonna have to leave everything behind. And it's all your daddy's fault."

"You're a cold-blooded snake, Trueblood," her father said, shoving the gambler aside. "Get away from my daughter."

Rafe chuckled and sauntered out the door, leaving his repulsive scent behind him. "Thanks for the ranch, Hollis," Rafe Trueblood called over his shoulder. "My family was needin' somewhere to live, and this place will do us fine."

"Daddy?" Deannie had whimpered, stunned and confused.

Her father had gone down on his knees in front of her, an agonized expression on his face. He had wrapped one arm around her and pulled her tight against his chest while his tears dampened her nightgown. "I'm sorry, baby, so sorry."

"Who is that man, Daddy? Why do we have to leave? Can I take my pony?"

"No, honey, you can't."

"Why?"

"Because, sweetheart, your daddy has gone and done a very stupid thing."

Down the hallway a door clicked closed, jerking Deannie from her terrible memory.

Brodie.

Deannie sat up and pushed her hair off her sweat-drenched forehead. The covers lay twisted around her legs, and her heart thundered harder than a West Texas hailstorm. Her mouth was dry and tasted chalky. Her hands trembled and her soul ached.

She glanced at her bedside travel clock. One-thirty. Was Brodie still awake? Obviously, he had his own demons.

For the first time in her life, Deannie felt a twinge of sympathy for a Trueblood. As fallible as her own father had been, at least at heart he had been a good person, whereas Rafe Trueblood had been a total blackguard through and through.

Imagine growing up with Rafe for a father. Childhood could not have been easy for Brodie either.

Swinging her legs over the edge of the bed, Deannie sat there a moment, trying to get her emotions under control before she trekked across the hallway to the bathroom. She panted against the thick, heavy sensation in her chest.

Coming back to Willow Creek had unearthed ugly memories and rock-hard emotions. She'd known returning would dredge up those dark feelings, but Deannie had to admit the actual reality was far more shocking than she'd expected.

She stared at the square of moonlight seeping through the window and onto the carpet. Fought hard to suppress the tears welling in her throat. Crying would get her nowhere. Pleading would do no good. Weeping, she'd discovered on that awful night so long ago, was for sissies.

Deannie clenched her jaw. Not she. She was not her father's daughter. She was a fighter, a survivor. She refused to give in to defeat no matter how the odds seemed stacked against her.

She would not fail. Somehow, someway, through hook or by crook, she would wrest Willow Creek Ranch back from the Truebloods if it took her dying breath to achieve her goal.

❧ 10 ❧

Deannie steered Brodie's four-wheel drive pickup truck across the back pasture. He had given her the keys that morning along with a hand-drawn map to help her locate the log cabin. She didn't need instructions. She remembered exactly where Papaw's old cabin sat nestled among the willow trees flanking the creek bank that was only full after the spring run off when the snow melted from the Davis Mountains.

Brodie promised to meet her at the cabin by nine o'clock to help her get things organized. With Emma scheduled to come home from the hospital tomorrow, they didn't have much time to get the place cleaned and readied for occupancy. Kenny had taken Angel and Buster into town with him, freeing Deannie to do the chores.

At breakfast, Brodie had acted pleasant if not quite friendly. Deannie accepted his mood, knowing she had to give him breathing room. Last night's events strengthened her resolve. She would wait forever if that's what it took to make Brodie Trueblood fall in love with her.

A roadrunner darted from the tall Johnson grass and raced along beside the truck as she guided the vehicle over rough brushy terrain. Cattle grazed on both sides of the makeshift road. White-faced Herefords on the left, Black Angus on the right. A windmill, old but still functional, spun listlessly beside the stock tank. Along the fence row, giant sunflowers grew in wild abandon.

Deannie rolled down the window and took in a deep breath of home. Scissortails flitted on the telephone lines, and killdeers cried from the ground beneath the mesquite trees. Nostalgia mixed with regret. The emotions rose inside her, knotting hard and pressing relentlessly against her rib cage until she had difficulty catching her breath.

She'd lost so much. Not just her home, but her heritage as well. When she should have been spending her childhood shinnying up trees and catching tadpoles in the pond, she'd been wandering through back alleys looking for aluminum cans to sell and sleeping on pool tables in smoky bars waiting for her daddy to cash in his chips and go home.

"Damn you, Rafe Trueblood, for stealing my life," Deannie muttered, fisting one hand in her lap. "But I'll have the last laugh."

And hurt Brodie in the process?

Those words floated through Deannie's mind, but she tamped them down along with her guilt. Brodie was a big boy, and he could take care of himself.

She drove over a rise and spotted Papaw's log cabin in the distance, partially hidden by willow trees.

The sight of it brought tears to Deannie's eyes, and she brushed them from her cheek. None of that, she chided herself, but her chest squeezed tighter.

She bumped across the trickling creek and rode over a clump of smooth, flat rocks. Brodie's truck easily scaled the craggy territory. It was a brand-new pickup, this year's model, complete with all the bells and whistles. Electric windows and doors, an expensive sound system and extended cab, reclining leather bucket seats.

Pulling up to the cabin, she sat there a moment, gathering her courage to face what lay ahead. Her gaze scanned the yard. Weeds had taken over the spot where her grandmother used to work a vegetable garden. Deannie could almost taste the vine-ripened tomatoes, crisp ears of baby corn, and savory black-eyed peas. Her mouth watered. Store-bought produce had never rivaled homegrown.

The front screen door hung on one hinge, and aged farming equipment rusted beside a decrepit chicken coop long since devoid of poultry. An old-fashioned hand pump was positioned over a water trough around the side of the house, a white salt lick squatting beside it. A few boards in the corral recently replaced, the bright-brown wood a stark contrast against the gray, weathered fencing.

Killing the engine, Deannie took a deep breath and got out of the truck. A jackrabbit leaped up from behind a cactus, tall ears twitching, his powerful hind legs propelling him across the prairie at lightning-quick speed.

Startled, Deannie stumbled backward, muttering under her breath. She should have worn boots instead of her sneakers. What if that rabbit had been a rattlesnake?

She glanced at her watch. Ten minutes until nine. Brodie would be here soon.

After retrieving cleaning supplies from the truck bed, Deannie headed up the stone path leading to the cabin. Juggling the mop, broom, bucket, soap, and bleach, she nudged the screen door open with her toe. The reluctant metal shrieked in protest.

A musty odor greeted her when she entered the cabin. A fine layer of dust covered everything—card board boxes, sheet-draped furniture, brown paper sacks, steamer trunks. The tiny house was jam-packed with junk. Evidently, Brodie used the cabin as storage space.

Whew. Deannie rested her hands on her hips and surveyed the clutter. They had their work cut out for them.

"Quite a mess, isn't it?"

The sound of Brodie Trueblood's voice sent chills rippling through her. Chills of desire, apprehension, or downright fear, Deannie couldn't say which. She set down the supplies and turned on her heels to face him.

Clearly, he had gotten little sleep. Dark circles ringed his eyes, and his cheeks appeared drawn and gaunt. He held his shoulders stiff, as if afraid to relax around her.

Even weary, he was still the handsomest man she'd ever seen. Not necessarily in the slick, polished way Hollywood defined as handsome. Brodie's attractiveness was much more than skin-deep. It was in the way he walked, the way he held himself. His voice, strong, deep, and masculine. And his slightly irregular features were far more intriguing than any flawless face.

"I didn't hear you drive up," Deannie said, nervously running a hand through her hair.

"I rode Ranger."

"Oh."

A curtain of silence settled over them. Deannie flicked her gaze around the room, desperately searching for something to focus on. Anything to keep from looking into Brodie's deep-brown eyes. Knowing eyes that seemed to peer straight into her soul.

Butterflies flitted in her stomach. She had to hold her goal firmly in mind—make Brodie fall in love with her. But she had to proceed carefully. Brodie's guard would be up. She had to find small ways to seduce him. Anything overt would send him running in the opposite direction.

Think, Deannie, what does Brodie care about? Willow Creek Ranch, Angel and Buster, Emma, his brother. Home and family. There lay the battlefield. If she were to win his heart, she had to appeal to his love for the land and his hunger for roots.

"We better get to work." Brodie nodded, all business, derailing her thoughts.

"Where do we start?" Deannie asked, overwhelmed.

"I'll stuff these boxes and crates into the bedrooms. That'll make room in here."

"What'll we do about the bedrooms?"

"Kenny can sleep on the fold-out couch."

"I think it's admirable," Deannie murmured, "what you're doing for your brother." She might deceive him, but she wasn't lying to him. She believed Brodie to be an honorable man.

So why are you so set on deceiving him?

Because there was no other way to get back Willow Creek. Damn, it was hard having a conscience. Too bad she wasn't as cold-blooded as Rafe. Actually, it was too bad Rafe wasn't alive, so she could get her revenge face-to-face and leave Brodie out of it all together.

Brodie didn't reply. Instead, he grasped a box and headed for the back room. Not knowing what else to do, Deannie gathered up two paper sacks and followed, knocking loose a dust shower.

The bedroom was small and almost as packed as the living room. It housed two twin beds stacked high with clutter. The peculiar assortment included Christmas decorations: multicolored twinkle lights, two plastic lawn Santas, a green and red felt tree skirt, yards and yards of unused

material in a variety of faded colors and moth-eaten fabrics, and a collection of Louis L'Amour paperbacks.

"Stack it anywhere." Brodie waved a hand.

"Where did this stuff come from?" Deannie asked, wrinkling her nose to suppress a sneeze.

"Most of it belonged to the previous owners."

Deannie froze, her fingers still curled around the sack. Some of her old possessions could be here?

"Some of it was my mother's..." Brodie's eyes fixed on an object in the corner, and his voice took on a husky tone and trailed off.

Deannie tracked his gaze and spied a carousel music box resting on top of an oak bureau.

He moved across the hardwood floor, his boots

making a rough clipping noise. His hand closed around the music box. He cradled it gently to his chest. In that moment, Deannie realized just how much his mother had meant to him.

His large fingers looked incongruous turning that tiny key. He wound it then set the music box back down on the bureau. She noticed he held his breath, and his hands trembled ever so slightly.

The music box sprang to life, the carousel horses twirling around the base as they moved up and down on their poles. A tinny melody filled the air, and Deannie cocked her head, trying to recognize the tune.

"'The Skater's Waltz.'"

The haunting chords echoed sadly throughout the room and tugged at her heart.

Brodie jammed his hands into his pockets and watched the carousel horses prance.

"My mother loved that music box," he whispered. "I bought it for her the Christmas I turned twelve. I mowed lawns all summer and raked leaves in the fall to pay for it."

His quiet revelation gave Deannie insight into him. Much-needed information she could use to draw closer to him. His mother had been the one to keep him stable. She had given him his strength of character. Her loving influence had prevented Brodie from taking after Rafe as Kenny had done.

Deannie cleared her throat. "Your mother must have meant a lot to you."

A hooded expression shuttered his eyes. "We were close."

"How did she die?"

"Cancer. She was only forty-two."

"I'm sorry."

Brodie raised his head and looked at her. She saw pain in his eyes. Deep, inconsolable. Even now.

"I built Willow Creek into what it is today as a tribute to her," he said. "You can see why this place means so much to me."

If only you knew how much this place means to me, too!

"Yes," Deannie replied. "I can understand. My mother died when I was seven."

"How?"

He'd warned her last night not to lie to him, but what could she do? If she told him her mother had been killed in a riding accident, he just might remember how Gil Hollis's wife died and put two and two together. He was already suspicious of her, and Brodie Trueblood was not a stupid man.

"She had cancer, too," she lied.

"So, you know how I feel." Compassion lit his eyes.

Deannie looked away, unable to bear Brodie's kindness.

Willow Creek had played an important role in both their lives. Coming to live here had given Brodie a sense of purpose, driving him to excel, while being torn from the ranch had given Deannie an equally insatiable desire to reclaim it as her own.

Walking the short distance across the cluttered room, she laid a hand on his shoulder. "I think your mother would be very proud of what you've done with Willow Creek."

Their gazes sealed. Something unspoken passed

between them. A silent recognition that bound them together.

"We better get to work." Brodie stepped back, dropping his gaze.

"Okay," she replied, yearning for something she couldn't quite name, and as he walked back outside, she couldn't help feeling she was on the verge of losing everything.

DESPITE HIS BEST INTENTIONS, HE WAS LETTING Deannie get too close. Brodie hefted another box onto his shoulder and carted it into the bedroom.

He couldn't afford to let things progress so swiftly. He didn't know enough about her, and what he knew was not very commendable.

"Cool your jets, Trueblood," he muttered under his breath. "There's plenty of time for things to develop. No hurry. No rush."

So why did a headlong urgency consume him? Why had thoughts of Deannie kept him awake all night? Why did he fantasize about the taste of those luscious pink lips when he fully knew of the dangers?

Yes, his head said, *Slow down, slow down, slow down.* But his body cried, *Now, now, now.*

Brodie stacked the box alongside the others, then placed his palms against his lower back and stretched.

Truthfully, he was feeling vulnerable. His father had just died, and even though they'd never seen eye to eye, a part of his past was dead and buried for good. Some mourning was expected.

Also, he was the one who had inherited Willow Creek. Complete responsibility for the ranch's success or failure lay at his feet. Brodie had to provide not only for himself but also for Kenny and his family.

There were adjustments and needs to satisfy. Needs that had been gnawing at Brodie for some time. A sharp, aching need to find a wife, get married, and have a family of his own. What was the point in pouring his heart into Willow Creek if he had no one to leave it to?

Brodie bit his bottom lip. How he longed for a chance to be a better father to his children than Rafe had been to him.

"Think about it later," he told himself.

"Did you say something?" Deannie inquired sweetly when he returned to the living room. She glanced up from where she was sweeping dust balls out the front door.

Mid-morning sunlight splashed into the cabin, catching her fiery red hair in a shining glow. She appeared almost angelic standing there with that halo of curls tumbling around her head, and the corners of her mouth tugged upward.

His stomach clenched in response to her smile. "Nothing," he mumbled.

The air smelled of soap and cleaning solution, and Brodie wondered if the smell might account for his dizziness. He wasn't admitting it was sexual chemistry.

She continued her sweeping, her lithe body moving in a hypnotic rhythm. *Whish, whish, whish.* The broom scooted across the wood.

They'd dressed like each other, Brodie noted with a start. Both were wearing white cotton T-shirts now streaked with dirt and faded blue jeans. The only difference was he had on boots and she'd donned sneakers. It was as if their minds ran along the same track. She was a feminine version of himself.

No. She's very different from you. Remember, you found her gambling in a bar. She's more like Kenny or Rafe.

Yet, Brodie couldn't shake the notion she was his female mirror image. His other half.

He watched Deannie, mesmerized by her lithe motion. How beguiling she looked, those faded denims hugging her fanny tighter than a lover's passionate embrace, her face scrubbed free of cosmetics. It took every ounce of control he could muster not to cross that floor, gather her into his arms, and kiss her.

Brodie didn't know how much more he could tolerate. How much longer could he keep his sanity? Yet, she'd done nothing to lead him on. It wasn't her fault. He couldn't toss her out on the streets.

"There," she said, rubbing her palms together. "That's a start."

"Huh?" He blinked, thankful she was unaware of the direction in which his mind traveled.

"I'll tackle the kitchen next. I've got an hour before I have to be back at the farmhouse to cook lunch."

Deannie tucked a lock of hair behind one perfect seashell-shaped ear, and that utterly innocent gesture had Brodie yearning to nibble her delectable lobes.

"Are you okay?" She squinted at him.

"Yeah. Fine." Nothing wrong except he was about to explode with desire. "Well, maybe the smell of cleaners is getting to me. Think I'll take a walk outside and get some fresh air."

"It is overpowering," Deannie agreed. "I'll open the windows."

Shaking his head, Brodie strode over to the corral where he'd tied Ranger. The gelding neighed a greeting.

Brodie scratched Ranger behind the ears. He glanced back over his shoulder at the cabin. She'd disappeared from the door, and he felt oddly lonesome.

When he'd told her about his mother, she'd listened quietly, a sad, pensive look upon her face. She'd been so receptive, he'd felt as if he could tell her anything. That alone was enough to scare the hell out of him. He'd always been closemouthed with his private thoughts. Why did he suddenly want to tell her everything?

Dang. He had to stop thinking about her like this. Maybe a ride around the perimeter would empty his head.

He swung into the saddle and wheeled Ranger west. The sun, perched high in the sky, beat down warm and cheerful. Brodie readjusted his hat to shade his eyes.

It wasn't fair to leave Deannie inside the cabin doing all the cleaning for his brother's benefit, but Brodie just could not face her at this moment. Not while they were out here all alone. One glance into those piercing eyes and he would be a goner for sure.

A bonus.

He would pay her a bonus to ease his conscience. Ranger tossed his head as if in agreement. Brodie kneed the gelding in the ribs, urging him into a trot. The horse surged forward. Grasshoppers sprang up in their wake. Brodie leaned low in the saddle, guiding Ranger toward the creek.

Brodie had come here often when the family had

first moved in at Willow Creek. The cabin, the creek, the willow trees had been his refuge from Rafe. That old familiar feeling of safety washed over him as Ranger traveled the creek bed, spindly willow branches slapping lightly against Brodie's legs.

Ranger's hooves kicked up a fine spray from the thin creek, splashing his face and cooling down the sizzle Deannie stirred inside him.

"He-ya!" Brodie called, gently kneeing the gelding.

Ranger sprang into a gallop. By this point, they had completely circled the cabin. Unable to stop himself, Brodie cast another glance at the front door.

And saw her.

Oblivious to him, Deannie was scrubbing the windows inside the cabin. The tip of her pink tongue caught between her teeth, and a narrow frown cut a path across her brow as she concentrated on the job.

Brodie stared.

Deannie stretched, reaching high to get the top panes. Her breasts, pert and firm, thrust forward, straining against her thin cotton T-shirt. Her nipples, hard as pebbles, pushing upward with the motion.

The sight generated a swift response. Immediate pressure rose below his belt, erecting an aching ballast against his zipper.

His mouth fell open. He gripped the saddle horn, and the reins slipped from his astonished fingers.

Ranger pitched up the creek bed, his hooves striking the rocks. Before Brodie could regain control, a tree branch whacked him in the face, knocking him off balance.

Brodie tumbled backward.

His arms flailed. His fingers grasped at air. He came up with a fistful of willow leaves and landed smack-dab on his backside.

In a cactus patch.

"Yeow!" Brodie howled.

His hat flew behind him. His boots hit the soft dirt, heels digging in deep. He tried to struggle to his feet but squirming only drove the spines deeper into his rear end. He stopped moving, panting against the pain.

Ranger stood there looking at him as if trying to figure out he'd managed to fall off.

"Brodie!" Deannie shouted. She dashed out the front door and ran toward him.

Strangely enough, just seeing her eased the sting. He watched her fly across the ground, with what he knew was a dopey expression on his face. Worry made her eyes shiny and her chest heave as she breathed rapid gasps.

"I saw you fall," she exclaimed when she reached him. "Are you all right?"

"Except for the cactus in my posterior, I'm fine."

"Oh, dear!" Deannie's eyes widened as she realized where he had landed.

Brodie extended her his hand. "Could you help me up, please?"

Nodding, she braced herself and tugged on his arm.

Brodie winced at the sharpness shooting through his backside. He pushed up, and she hauled him to his feet.

She took a step around him and stared down at his bottom. "Oh, my gosh," she whispered. "You're covered in thorns."

"Tell me about it," Brodie muttered.

Peeking back at his face, her mouth widened into a circle of concern. "What are we going to do?"

"There's a first aid kit in the pickup. Hopefully, there are some tweezers in it."

Brodie took a stiff step forward. A thousand tiny stickers pricked his skin. He hissed in a deep breath, excruciatingly aware of the embarrassing nature of his situation. Deannie would have to pluck the thorns from his butt.

Groaning more from that thought than from the pain, Brodie took another step.

"Goodness." Deannie laid her palms on either side of her cheeks in a gesture of disquiet. "I can't hardly stand to watch you."

"Aw," he said. "I've been through much worse than this."

Quit sniveling, Trueblood, and get over to the cabin. He couldn't have Deannie thinking him a wimp.

Mentally cinching himself against the pain, he set his jaw. He marched to the cabin, head held high. His blue jeans chafing against the bristles with every movement, Brodie swore under his breath.

"I'll get the first aid kit," Deannie volunteered and hurried over to the truck.

The pickup's door slammed behind him, and Deannie's feet slapped against the stone sidewalk as she caught up with him.

"Got it," she said.

He nodded, not really in the mood for conversation.

"Where are we gonna do this?" Deannie asked when they were inside the cabin. Brodie blinked in the dim coolness that contrasted with the brightness outside and the throbbing in his rear end.

Closing his eyes briefly, Brodie gulped. Where indeed?

"The couch will do," he replied, surprised to hear his words sound strangled. Whether it was from the pain or from what was about to happen next, he couldn't say.

Deannie tightened her hand around the first aid kit and made a face. "How are we going to get your pants off?"

"Do I have to take them off?"

"Brodie, how do you expect me to pluck those spines out through denim?" She had a point.

He sighed. "I don't want to expose myself."

"I know this isn't pleasant, but I'm the only one here to do it. You can't climb back on Ranger or ride in the truck to the farmhouse. Can you imagine bumping across the fields in your condition?"

Brodie gritted his teeth. No, he couldn't. "All right. I'll try to get the jeans off."

"While you're at it, I'll check the first aid kit for tweezers," she said.

"Good idea." Feeling like an A-number-one fool, Brodie turned his back to her and reached for his belt buckle.

Deannie focused her gaze on the first aid kit. Her vision narrowed to the large red cross gracing the front of the white plastic box. All moisture dried from her mouth.

Her eyes might have fixed on that kit as if it were a lifeline, but her ears attuned to every noise Brodie made from across the room. Crazy, seductive, getting-naked noises.

The sound of his belt unbuckling sent shivers skating down her spine. She heard the belt slither as he whipped it from the loops. Next came the snap. It popped as loud as a firecracker in her sensitive ears.

His zipper, easing down the track inch by painful inch, made a whispering noise that whooshed in her ears like the wild ocean tide during a lunar eclipse. Heat swamped her entire body. She was about to see Brodie's bare behind in all its radiant glory.

Oh dear, oh dear, oh dear. What had she gotten herself

into? Truth was, she'd never seen a naked man. This would be a first for her.

Deannie's fingers fumbled with the first aid kit's clasp. The ornery thing wouldn't budge. Her hands were thick with sweat, and a trickle of perspiration rolled down her cheek, plopping onto her shirt.

Calm down, chill out, cool it.

"You find the tweezers?" Brodie asked.

"Uh, I'm just having a little trouble getting this thing open. Are you ready?"

"I have to shimmy my jeans down."

At that visual image, she yanked on the lock and the kit sprang open, sending gauze and scissors and ointment flying across the room. Scrambling along the floor on her hands and knees in pursuit of the escaping supplies, she finally located the tweezers peeking out from under the edge of the couch.

"Got 'em." She waved the tweezers in the air.

"Let's get this over with," Brodie said grimly.

Deannie kept her head turned while Brodie carefully shucked his jeans. He groaned a couple of times, but all in all he handled it well.

"Ready," he said, sounding edgy and breathless.

She turned to find him lying on his stomach across the couch, his underwear still on. Thank heavens.

He wore bright-red bikini briefs. Deannie had to slap a hand over her mouth to keep from guffawing. She would never have figured straitlaced Brodie Trueblood as a man who favored bikini briefs.

Especially red ones.

Obviously, he had a deeply sensual side she would

never have guessed at. "Are you going to leave your underwear on?"

"Um...is it okay if I do?"

Way more than okay.

Relief poured through her. "I'll see if I can get the thorns out without you having to remove them." She didn't think she could survive seeing that firm butt completely unclothed. "I'm gonna need more light."

"There's a lamp in the bedroom."

"Be right back," she said, willing her heart to stop racing.

She hurried to the bedroom, retrieved the lamp, then returned to plug it in next to the sofa. She dropped to her knees beside him, her eyes level with his distracting fanny. Squinting, she gazed along those finely honed muscles.

"Oh, my."

"What is it?"

"There sure are lots. I don't know where to pluck first."

"For pity's sake, Deannie, grab one and yank it out," he said, his voice muffled from having his face thrust into the couch cushion. "They hurt like hell."

Her fingers quivered as she grasped the tweezer. Leaning over, she rested her elbow on the back of his knees to stabilize her hand. Squinting, she inspected his bottom.

The fine white quills stood out against the red cotton material. There were dozens. Over a hundred even. This could take forever. Deannie gulped.

Despite her best intentions to concentrate on the job at hand, she couldn't help noticing his finely corded legs and how his thighs curved enticingly into his hips. He smelled rather delicious, too, like leather and sand and horses. Most definitely the aroma of home. The scent she'd craved for the past fifteen years.

"Deannie?" he mumbled. "Is something wrong?"

"I'm scared of hurting you."

"Just do it." He sounded rather irritated.

"Okay. Here goes nothing."

Tweezers posed, she jerked out an offending spine.

Brodie grunted. "Keep going."

Depositing it into the lid of the first aid kit, Deannie then tackled another one.

His skin burned warm beneath her arm. The hair on his legs glowed dark and thick. Deannie tried not to notice such things, but it was impossible.

She forgot to breathe.

Her entire body underwent an incredible metamorphosis. Her head swam. Her pulse sped up. Her nipples hardened. Her tummy melted. Her toes curled and her heart sang.

One thought and one thought only pounded in her brain.

I want to make love to Brodie Trueblood.

❦

BRODIE WAS IN AGONY. NOT FROM THE CACTUS spines, but from Deannie's hot breath torching a hole through his posterior. He couldn't stand much more of this.

It was a darn good thing he was lying on his stomach, or she would be very shocked to discover exactly what thoughts were bouncing around his head, causing some very physical reactions.

Her soft skin brushing against the back of his legs, her glorious magnolia scent badgering his nostrils, the quiet little tsk-tsking sounds she made with her tongue drove him batty.

Remember, Trueblood, you can't let your hormones rule your head.

Then a startling notion hit him. What if Deannie felt the same way about him? What if she were hesitant to acknowledge *her* feelings because she worried where it might lead?

Closing his eyes, Brodie groaned into the pillow.

Deannie hissed in a breath. "I'm sorry. Did I hurt you?"

"Don't stop." It already seemed as if they'd been here for eons, he wanted this over and done with.

"I got all the big ones, but there are still lots of little ones I can barely see through your underwear."

She ran a finger over the spot where the thorns were thickest. A million pinpricks shot through his nerve endings.

"Ouch!" He arched his back against the pain. "What are you doing?"

"I'm feeling them since I can't see." She sounded frustrated.

It probably wasn't much easier for her than it was for him.

"Easy does it," he urged. "Easy."

"Brodie," Deannie said huskily, "there's simply no way around it. I'm going to have to push your underwear out of the way to get the rest."

He gritted his teeth. "Do what you have to do."

Her nimble fingers curled around the elastic at his leg. Her fingernails lightly scratched the area where his thigh merged with his buttocks. Awareness fused with discomfort, and Brodie wondered whether he had died, and this was his punishment in hell—a beautiful, sexy woman raising his undies so she could pick stickers from his bare rump.

"There," she said, "that's much better."

He could tell she was keeping the cotton material pushed upward with one hand while she continued to extract thorns with the other. He'd never been in a more embarrassing situation.

The overhead ceiling fan blew cool air against his bare skin, but Brodie burned so hot inside, he scarcely noticed.

Time stretched, elongating into slow motion. He experienced each of Deannie's measured movements in excruciating minutiae. The tip of the metal tweezers poked and prodded. Her breath whistled softly as she inhaled through clenched teeth. Her aroma, like large white flowers blooming in the spring sunshine, over-whelmed his senses.

"I think I got them all," she crowed, triumphant at last.

Hallelujah!

"Here, let me check." Tentatively, Brodie reached a hand around behind him and gingerly fingered his rear end. The area was raw, tender, but he felt no more prickles.

Deannie had rocked back on her heels and was

observing him, while still holding his underwear aloft for his explorations.

His finger struck something. "There's one."

"Hang on, I'll get it."

A twinge, then it was gone.

"Check again," she said.

"You got them all."

"Now for the antibiotic ointment," she said.

"I'll do it," Brodie said, hastily taking the ointment from her. He applied it quickly and then pushed himself to a sitting position.

Deannie moved to sit beside him. "Still sore."

"It's fine." Knowing his face was as crimson as his underwear, Brodie avoided meeting her eyes. "Thanks. I know it wasn't pleasant for you, either."

"Oh, I don't know about that," she drawled, the sound of her voice sending a shudder through his groin. "I've certainly had worse chores."

Holy smokes! He was getting in even deeper.

"Don't be embarrassed, Brodie. It could happen to anyone."

"Well," he drawled, "this wasn't the way I imagined you'd get to see my backside."

"No?"

He sneaked a fast peek at her and saw a teasing smile curl her lips. One cocky eyebrow perched on her forehead, and her eyes danced with mirth.

"No." He laughed, helpless to resist her.

"How *did* you imagine it?"

"Um...er...you know," he stammered and ducked his head. "I better get dressed." He reached across the floor for his jeans.

"Wait a minute; there might be some thistles in your jeans," she cautioned. "Let me check them for you."

He handed her his pants and settled back down on the couch. He wanted to pace the floor, to thread his fingers through his hair, to dash from the room, anything to ease the riot in his brain.

But he couldn't. He had no pants.

Deannie held his jeans under the lamp, squinting and running her fingers lightly across the seat, intently searching for cactus thorns.

Watching, Brodie gulped.

Her mouth twisted into a studious expression, her curly red hair trailing down her shoulders, her slender fingers moving gracefully.

Brodie remembered his mother sitting in her favorite chair at night, doing the mending. They didn't have money for new clothes; their outfits were hand-me-downs from neighbors or stuff Mama picked up at Goodwill or the Salvation Army. Consequently, most of the garments required repair—hems taken up, buttons sewn on, rips patched.

An overwhelming tenderness swept over Brodie as he watched Deannie. Before he could stop himself, before he could think twice, Brodie leaned over and kissed her.

Lightly, gently, sweetly on the cheek.

Deannie looked up, surprise widening her eyes.

Whisked away on the moment, Brodie put his arm around her and drew her closer. Sitting there in his underwear, he felt vulnerable yet strangely free as if his inhibitions had disappeared along with the cactus quills.

Deannie smelled so fine, felt so good in his embrace,

he had to taste her. Dipping his head, he angled for her lips.

That mouth, soft and inviting, lured him forward.

Her teeth parted slightly, and she closed her eyes.

With a hungry growl, he claimed her mouth. Closing his eyes against the onslaught of sensations zipping through his system, Brodie clung to her, drinking her delicious nectar.

No woman had ever made him feel so vibrant, so masculine, so alive. For twenty-nine years, he'd been trapped inside a cage of his own making, and Deannie had just produced a key and swung open the doors of his prison.

He kissed her again and again.

She was so responsive! A little moan escaped her lips, and she wriggled closer, her thigh rubbing against his bare leg.

"Oh." She sighed long and deep and dreamy. "Brodie."

He cupped her cheeks in his palms, and she opened her mouth wider, letting him come as far in as he wanted. Her moistness fed him. Stoked his excitement. It was as if he'd spent his whole life eating peanut butter and stale crackers when he could have been dining on lobster, steak, and caviar.

His whole life narrowed to the focus of that sweet mouth. On her. This woman who strolled into his life and changed everything overnight.

Deannie pressed both palms against his chest and pushed gently. "Why?"

Brodie drew back. "Why what?"

"Why did you kiss me?"

"I like you, Deannie. I like you a lot."

Tears misted her eyes, and she lowered her head. Was she going to cry? Why? He hadn't meant to upset her.

"Deannie?" He reached out, cupped her chin in his hand, and eased her face upward until she looked him in the eyes. "Are you angry with me?"

She shook her head, and her eyes looked impossibly sad. Why? "No."

"What's wrong?"

"Nothing." Her body stiffened.

"Talk to me...please."

"You're so nice," she whispered. "Too nice."

"That's a problem?"

She shook her head again. "You don't understand."

"Tell me."

"I'm not..." She inhaled deeply. "It can't..."

"Were you in an abusive relationship before?" The thought someone had mistreated her jammed his gut with anger, and he knotted his fists.

"No."

"Come on," he coaxed, reaching up to wipe away the tear that slid down her cheek. "Tell me."

"There's nothing to tell." She dropped her hands into her lap and stared down at them.

He didn't want to badger her, but he could tell something heavy weighed on her mind. He rubbed a knuckle along her cheek, and a shiver ran through him. Her skin was so soft. "Deannie? What is it?"

"Don't lead me on, Brodie," she said.

"What do you mean?"

"You're running hot and cold. One minute you want

to keep your distance. The next you're—" She swept a hand at him sitting there in his underwear.

He stared at her.

She had a point. Deannie blinked at him. He could see the pulse pounding at the vein in the hollow of her throat.

He'd been waffling, sending mixed messages. Last night he'd issued his hands-off policy; today he'd sneaked a kiss. He blamed it on the cactus thorns. *Not owning your part in this, huh, Trueblood? Man up. You escalated things.*

"You're right," he said. "I apologize. I was way out of line."

"Not way out of line." She offered a small smile. "But..."

"But?"

"It's not that I don't like kissing you. I do. Very much. That's the problem. When you kiss me... I want more." She paused, then lowered her voice so he could barely hear her. "So very much more."

A car horn tooted outside the cabin. They both jumped. Brodie vaulted off the couch, yanked on his jeans, and hurried to the window. It was his brother's pickup truck, Angel and Buster in the back seat.

"Who is it?" she asked.

"Kenny and the kids."

"Oh heavens," she said, hopping up and brushing back hair that had fallen across her face. "We're nowhere near ready."

No, no, they were not.

She was talking about the cabin, but it applied just

as well to their runaway chemistry. And she was dead right too.

Here was the kicker though. While they might not be ready for what was unfolding between them, it seemed to happen anyway.

Vehicle doors slammed. Children's voices filled the air.

She turned away, opened the door, and welcomed his family inside.

12

The next day, Buster, Angel, Deannie, and Brodie brought Emma and the new baby home from the hospital. Ensconced in the cabin with a sober companion Brodie hired for him on his road to sobriety, Kenny stayed behind. He'd attend AA meetings twice a day in Rascal with the sober companion and spend his time putting a new roof on the cabin.

Deannie and Brodie hadn't spoken since his brother and the children had interrupted them the morning before. In fact, they'd been avoiding each other. Brodie had taken his dinner in Rascal instead of dining with her and the kids and the ranch hands.

What happened between them in the cabin shook her to the core.

Why did she go soft and melting inside every time she glimpsed him riding across the field? Why did her heart jackhammer when she heard his voice? Why did the guilt she fought so hard to suppress come swinging back with a vengeance, her conscience nagging her day and night to reconsider her plan to marry Brodie?

Now, Deannie waited in the back seat of Emma's SUV. Buster and Angel were in third row seating behind her. An empty third car seat, where the new baby would ride, was strapped into the seat across from Deannie. Brodie had gone inside to check Emma out of the hospital and left the engine running so they'd have air conditioning. The children chattered excitedly and bounced up and down in their car seats.

"I get to hold him first," Buster announced. "'Cause I'm the big brother."

"Nuh-uh." Angel thrust her bottom lip out in a pout. "I getta ho'd him first."

"Deannie," Buster said. "Tell her she's too little to hold the baby."

"Am not!" Angel got out of her car seat and dove at her brother with her fists flailing.

"Shh, shh," Deannie whispered. "Do you want your mother to find you fighting?"

"No, ma'am," Buster said solemnly.

"No, 'am," Angel echoed.

"Let's play a game," she said. "Have you ever played I Spy?"

"Uh-huh." Angel bobbed her head.

"I spy with my li'l eye." Buster pointed. "*Tilda*."

Deannie glanced at the hospital entrance, and there stalking the sidewalk, was Brodie's former housekeeper, Matilda Jennings.

The minute the gray-haired woman spotted the SUV she marched over.

"Me no wike her," Angel whimpered.

Me either, Deannie thought.

Matilda, her sourpuss face drawn into a hard frown, rapped on the window.

Reluctantly, Deannie put the window down.

"Well, well, well, if it isn't Miss Priss."

Forcing a smile, Deannie said, "Good morning."

"You're not fooling me. I know you're up to no good." Matilda shook a finger under Deannie's nose. "And I'm gonna keep after you until I figure out what game you're playing. Brodie might be a trusting fool, but I ain't."

"Excuse me," Deannie said, her stomach roiling. "The cool air is getting out." She leaned over to put the window back up.

"Not so fast." Matilda slapped her palm over the rim of the window glass. "I'm not done with you yet."

"What is it?" Deannie dropped her smile. The woman knew nothing, otherwise she would already have gone to Brodie with her suspicions.

Matilda's eyes gleamed. "I want in on the action."

"There is no *action*."

"Don't yank my chain. You're angling to get that man to marry you so you can run herd over Willow Creek. If I was twenty years younger, I'd pull the same stunt myself."

Fear jelled Deannie's veins, but she wasn't about to let the woman see her sweat. "I do not understand what you're talking about."

"Lie through your teeth all you want, girlie. I learned the real scoop from some of those fellas you played poker with at the Lonesome Dove. Just remember, I'm on to you, and I intend on either getting my job back or making a pile of money off you."

"Are you threatening me, Mrs. Jennings?" Deannie put the smile back on, this time injecting it with steel. She put on a brave front, but her insides were liquid terror. "Last time I checked, blackmail was against the law."

"So is defrauding people."

"I have defrauded no one. If you'll please take your hand off the door, I'd like to put up the window."

"You haven't seen the last of me," Matilda warned. "I'll be in touch." With that, the iron-jawed woman strutted away leaving Deannie quaking all over.

What if Matilda made good on her threats and dug around until she found out she was really Deanna Hollis? Although Deannie had been very careful. She purposely stayed off all social media, striving to keep her digital footprint as small as possible.

"Look," Buster said. "There's Mama."

"Where?" Angel pressed her face against the window that Deannie had just raised.

Sucking in air Deannie stared at Brodie as he came down the walkway, carrying a bundle wrapped in a blue blanket. A smiling dark-haired woman seated in a wheel-chair at his side, wheeled along by a hospital attendant.

When they reached the SUV parked in the passenger loading zone, Brodie opened the front passenger side door, and the attendant helped Emma inside.

Then he came around to strap the newborn into the car seat beside Deannie.

For once, Angel and Buster were silent. Their eyes

loomed wide in their faces, and their mouths hung open as they leaned over the seat to see the newest Trueblood.

Deannie, still shaken from her encounter with Matilda, kept her hands in her lap and her body perfectly still. Everything had changed. Before Matilda's threat, Deannie expected plenty of time to woo Brodie. But now she could no longer afford the luxury of time.

"This is my br...bro...brother?" Buster stammered.

"Yes, honey," Emma turned to smile at her oldest child and glimpsed Deannie. She winked. "Hi, I'm Emma, and I'm assuming you are Deannie. Brodie's told me so much about you. He says you're amazing with the kids."

It was impossible not to return Emma's engaging grin. Despite the anxiety crawling through her stomach, Deannie smiled back. "Your kids are the amazing ones, and they keep me on my toes."

"Oh." Emma chuckled. "I see you know my children."

"Kisses, Mommy, kisses." Angel broke free from her car seat and surged to where her mother sat, climbing over Deannie and the new baby to get there, puckering her lips for maternal kisses.

"Me too, me too." Buster came out of his car seat too and joined his sister, the kids' chubby little legs brushing against Deannie as they leaned in for their mother's attention.

"Okay, okay, back to your seats," Deannie said, "so we can get your mommy home. Then you can have all the hugs and kisses you want."

She got the kids buckled into their seats, and Brodie got behind the wheel.

Emma smiled at Deannie in the rearview mirror and mouthed, *Thank you.*

Leaving Deannie feeling a half dozen conflicting things all at once.

HELPLESSLY, DEANNIE STARED AT BRODIE AS HE helped Emma from the SUV once they were back at Willow Creek Ranch. She'd just gotten Angel and Buster out and turned back to see who would take the new baby.

She took in the firm, clean lines of his broad shoulders and his straight posture. He tugged his Stetson lower over his forehead and turned to get the baby. Cradling the infant against the crook of his elbow as if holding a newborn was the most natural thing in the world, he passed his nephew to his mother.

"Does anyone want to see the baby?" Emma asked.

"Oh, yes, Mommy, pwease." Angel clapped her hands, and Emma unwrapped the wriggly little package in her arms.

Buster closed one eye and assessed his baby brother. "He's tiny, Mama. You sure we shouldn't throw him back and wait 'til he's bigger?"

Brodie chuckled. "That works on fish, buddy, not babies."

"Why don't we go inside?" Deannie suggested, seeing how pale and worn Emma looked.

"Good idea." Emma smiled at her again.

"Me got the prettiest baby in the who'e wor'd," Angel cooed, slipping her hand into Deannie's and skipping along beside her as they headed inside the house.

"Yes, you do," Deannie agreed. Darn. There it was again. That deep pang of something important missing from her life.

Once in the house, Emma went into the living room and sat down, resting the baby on her thighs while Buster and Angel plopped on either side of their mother, both talking at once. Emma peeled off the baby's socks and counted his toes, a happy Madonna smile on her lips.

Buster said, "This little piggy went to market."

"Roast beef!" Angel giggled.

"Is there anything I can get for you?" Deannie asked. "Something to drink? Are you hungry?"

"No, thank you," Emma smiled. "I'm fine for now."

"The new baby is very handsome."

"Would you like to hold him while I cuddle these two?" Emma asked.

Deannie laid a hand on her chest. "Me?"

"Sure." Emma extended the baby toward her.

"B-but I've never held a baby before," Deannie stammered.

"Nothing to it. Just support his head like this. See?"

"What if I drop him?" she whispered, drawing closer.

"You won't."

Tentatively, Deannie reached out and took the newborn from his mother's arms. He opened his eyes and peered at her, fuzzy and unfocused.

Awed, Deannie stared at his tiny hands. His face

was slightly red and his features scrunchy, but Phillip Brodie Trueblood was the most adorable thing she'd ever seen.

"It's amazing," she said, not knowing what else to say.

"I know." A satisfied smile warmed Emma's brown eyes. "Just wait until you have your own."

Deannie shook her head. "I'm not sure I'll ever have children."

Emma's mouth formed a stunned circle. "Why not?"

"The world's a pretty rough place, why bring a child into it?"

"Because babies are our hope for the future," Emma murmured.

"It's too bad," Deannie said, "that his father isn't here to enjoy the moment." Her statement obliterated the joy from Emma's face, and she wished she could have bitten off her tongue. That was a mean thing to say. Why had she said it?

"Yes," Emma said tightly, casting glances at the other two children snuggling against her. "It is bad when their father won't grow up and assume responsibility for his family."

"I'm sorry," Deannie apologized. "I spoke out of turn. I shouldn't have said that."

"You said nothing that wasn't true."

"It might be true, but it was unkind. Please forgive me."

"What's true?" Buster perked up.

"Nothing, darling. Why don't you take your sister and go get a diaper out of the diaper bag for me. Can you do that for Mommy?"

"You betcha." In an instant Buster was on his feet. "C'mon, Angel, let's go."

Angel, for once in an acquiescent mood, took her brother's hand and followed him out of the room.

"Have a seat." Emma patted the couch cushion beside her where Buster had been sitting. "Even though he's tiny, it doesn't take long for him to get heavy."

Deannie sank down next to Emma. The baby yawned widely and rubbed at his face with his little fists.

"I have to watch what I say about Kenny in front of the kids. Little pitchers have big ears. They'll be right back."

"If you don't want to talk about it, I understand. Really, it's none of my business," Deannie replied, surprised at how frank and open Emma was about her marriage. "But Brodie told me you and Kenny were getting divorced, and I couldn't help but think that was such a shame. You with a new baby and all."

Emma gulped, and Deannie could tell she was fighting tears. "Actually, it's good to have someone to talk to. Most of my family lives in Midland, and though we've only just met, I have a feeling you and I will be great friends."

"You do?"

Emma nodded. "Brodie sure was singing your praises."

"Really?" Deannie ducked her head.

"He likes you."

"I like him, too."

"He's a good man. Not at all like Rafe, and I hate to say it, my husband."

"What do you mean?" Deannie asked, knowing exactly what Emma meant. She was far too familiar with the flaws of the Trueblood clan, but Emma didn't know that.

Emma sighed. "Rafe, Brodie and Kenny's dad, was larger than life; he could charm a raccoon out of a tree. But he was real polecat. He drank and gambled and chased women and broke his wife's heart. Both Brodie and Kenny believe his behavior is what drove their mother to an early grave."

"How awful."

"Did you hear the story of how Rafe got his hands on a place like Willow Creek?"

Deannie shook her head.

"He won it in a poker game like some Wild West outlaw. Do you know what else he did?"

"No," Deannie said in a quiet whisper, the sleeping baby heavy in her arms.

"He threw the real owner of the ranch out on the street in the middle of the night. The man and his seven-year-old daughter." Emma clicked her tongue. "What kind of person does such a heartless thing?"

Deannie froze at Emma's words. What kind of person indeed?

"I didn't know Rafe back then. Apparently, he'd mellowed a lot by the time I came on the scene. You couldn't help but like him, he was so friendly, but you knew never to trust him with your money."

"I don't even see how you could like such a man."

"Oh, you know," Emma waved a hand. "Rafe was a big flirt. Always paying compliments. Kenny took after him. He swept me off my feet. I was young. He was a motorcycle-riding bad boy. So exciting for a mousy minister's daughter. By the time I realized that Kenny was never going to grow up, I was madly in love with him and two months pregnant with Buster."

Deannie said nothing. What could she say?

"Things were fantastic in the beginning. Kenny attempted to settle down. He took a job in the oil fields. We rented a little two-bedroom house on Pinion Street. Sure, Kenny went out on Friday nights with his buddies, but I didn't mind. He was bringing home good money, and we had everything we needed."

"So, what happened?"

Emma sighed and toyed with a loose thread on her blouse. "After Angel was born, oil prices dipped, and Kenny got laid off."

Deannie made sympathetic noises.

"He came to work for Brodie here at the ranch. But Kenny wanted to be the boss, and of course, Willow Creek is Brodie's baby. He's made this ranch what it is today. Not Rafe, not Kenny."

And not my father." Must have been hard for all of you."

"Kenny came to work drunk one time too many, and Brodie fired him."

"Ouch."

"He offered to let us live here, but Kenny wouldn't hear of it. That's when things got bad. Kenny would hang out at the Lonesome Dove, drinking and gambling away our savings. If I said anything to him, he would fly into a rage and call me a nagging shrew." Emma's bottom lip trembled.

"You don't have to say any more." Deannie patted the other woman's arm.

"I think I need to talk about it. To figure out what went wrong. I will say one thing for Kenny; I know he never cheated on me. At least I haven't had to bear *that* cross." Emma laced her fingers together and was silent for a moment.

Deannie craned her neck to see into the other room. Where had Buster and Angel gotten off to? They should be back by now.

"Then Rafe died, and the stuff really hit the fan."

"What do you mean?"

"Rafe had been sick with liver failure for several months. We all knew it was getting near the end. I think Kenny had been counting on an inheritance to bail us out."

Deannie said nothing.

"Turns out Rafe left everything to Brodie. Nobody was more shocked than Kenny. He and Rafe had been tight. They partied together, understood each other. I imagine Kenny thought he'd inherit Willow Creek over Brodie."

The clock on the mantel ticked loudly in the still room. Only the sound of the baby's soft breathing disrupted the silence.

"Kenny went off the deep end after that. We had a terrible fight, and I left him. Brodie invited me to stay here until I can figure out what I want to do."

"And you've decided on divorce?"

"Deannie, what else can I do? I refuse to live the way Melinda lived all those years, loving a man who was so selfish he thought only of himself. I might have made some big mistakes in my life, but I'm not a total fool."

Deannie squeezed Emma's hand, still worrying about the kids. "I'm so sorry."

Emma wiped an errant tear from her eye. "It's hard, you know. Dealing with all this when you're pregnant."

"I can only imagine." Deannie shook her head again.

"I still love Kenny. But I can't take him back until he proves he's willing and able to change for good. I've had enough. There's only so much a woman can be expected to accept."

"Where did those kids get off to?" Deannie muttered.

"My goodness, I'm so out of it." Emma shook her head. "I'd forgotten I sent them off on a mission."

"I'll go look." Deannie handed Emma the baby, but before she could leave the room, the kids came back in.

"Hey, Mama, we cou'dn't finded no diaper bag in the mud room so we went upstairs," Angel said, bouncing into the room ahead of her brother.

Buster was scratching his head and looking puzzled.

"What's the matter, son?" Emma asked, pasting a smile on her face.

"How come Uncle Brodie's packing a suitcase?" Buster sank his hands on his little hips.

Emma arched an eyebrow and looked at Deannie.

Deannie shrugged. Brodie was leaving?

Brodie appeared at the top of the stairs, two suit-cases clutched in his hands.

"What's happening?" Emma demanded, staring at her brother-in-law.

"Uh...well...I thought I'd give you ladies the run of the house," he said.

"What do you mean?" Emma said. "Where are you going?"

Brodie carefully avoided Deannie's gaze. "With a new baby in the house, I thought you'd need your space. So I figured I'd hole up in the old log cabin for a few weeks."

"That's absurd. I'm not turning you out of your house."

"Please, Emma, it's as much your house as it is mine," he insisted.

"Brodie..."

"I just need a little privacy."

"I see." Emma chuckled. "You don't want to be around for those two a.m. feedings and diaper changes."

Brodie headed out the door. Deannie felt a sudden urge to intercept him and find out what was going on. She followed him.

"What's this all about?" she asked, sinking her hands on her hips as he tossed his suitcases into the bed of the pickup truck.

He avoided looking at her. "Kenny's sober companion had a family emergency, and he needs me to help him stay on the straight and narrow. Please don't tell Emma where he's at."

"Is that the only reason you're running away?" she asked. "Couldn't you just hire Kenny another sober companion?"

Brodie climbed into the cab and slammed the door shut. "What do you want me to say, Deannie? That after what happened yesterday, I can't trust myself to keep my hands off you?"

"Is it the truth?"

He captured her eyes with his. "What do you think?"

A thrill hurdled through her. Things were changing between them, shifting and evolving into something deep and complicated.

"Would you like me to leave Willow Creek?" she asked.

"No." His response was swift and unequivocal. "You need a place to stay, and Emma needs someone to help her. She's going to be upset when Kenny doesn't come around for a while."

"What about you, Brodie? What do you need?"

His eyes darkened. "I need you, Deannie. So badly I can taste it. That's why I can't stay in the same house with you. We don't know enough about each other, and I'd hate for either of us to suffer third-degree burns from this runaway blaze between us."

That startled her. She watched as he threw the truck into gear and backed out of the driveway. Had she gotten to him? Her heart pitched at the thought. The answer, it seemed, was yes.

Only trouble was, he'd gotten to her, too!

13

Seeing Deannie holding his baby nephew had done something crazy to Brodie's brain. She looked sweet, so maternal that for one crazy moment, he'd pretended she was holding their baby.

What the heck was that all about?

It was a damn good thing the sober companion had a family emergency. It made for a handy excuse to leave. But even before that, he'd already decided to clear out of the house. Whenever he was around her, he ached to scoop her into his arms, take her into his bedroom, and make love to her all night long.

It was too soon in their tenuous relationship for him to get this twisted up. Besides, a few weeks in Kenny's company might do them both a world of good. Perhaps they could take a stab at repairing the rift between them.

Killing the engine outside the log cabin, Brodie waved a hand to Kenny, who was busy putting on a new screen door.

"Hey, little brother." Kenny stopped working, ran the back of his hand across his forehead, and approached the truck. "How's Emma?"

"She's fine."

"And the baby?"

"He's a good-looking boy." Brodie got his suitcases out of the truck.

"What's this?"

"I'm replacing your sober companion."

"You don't have to babysit me. I'm finished with drinking for good, and I mean it. Losing my wife brought me to my senses. I don't intend to end up like the old man."

"It's not just about you."

"No?"

"I need somewhere to stay."

Kenny whistled long and low, then grinned. "It's that redhead, isn't it?"

Brodie didn't answer.

"It is the redhead. Are you falling for her?"

"I'm not falling for her," Brodie denied, but his pulse sped up.

"I'll be damned. I never thought ol' stony-hearted Brodie would fall in love," Kenny teased.

"I'm not in love with her."

"Yeah, keep telling yourself that."

"I'm not."

Kenny raised both palms. "Hey, I'm not looking for a fight."

"Then stop picking one."

"Sure *you* don't have a hangover?"

"You know I don't drink."

"Do your feelings have anything to do with what happened yesterday when me and the kids caught you alone out here with her?"

"I told you what happened." Brodie denied, but who was he kidding? He *was* falling for Deannie. "There's nothing going on between us."

"Oh, that's right. Cactus in the backside. A likely story."

"It's true—" Brodie broke off, realizing Kenny was trying to get a rise out of him.

Kenny snorted.

"Why are you giving me a hard time? You're the one in the hot seat." He slung his arm over Kenny's shoulders.

"Go ahead, rub it in." Grumbling good-naturedly, Kenny followed him into the cabin.

It had been a long time since they'd kidded each other like this.

All at once, a joyful feeling lifted Brodie's spirits. He couldn't remember when he'd felt so optimistic. Things seemed to fall into place at last. His brother had finally recognized his problem and was seeking help. His father had bequeathed him a thriving ranch, and the most beautiful woman in the world was living in his house.

Brodie Trueblood was on the verge of having his every dream fulfilled at last. He needed a little patience and a little perseverance, but that was okay.

He had all the time in the world.

MAY FLOWED INTO JUNE, THEN JUNE SPILLED OVER into July. The temperature flared hotter; the grass burned drier. Peaches clinging to the backyard trees went from hard green knots to lush ripe fruit that fell readily into waiting palms. Emma's baby grew healthy and happy with constant attention.

But with each passing day, Deannie's heart sank heavier.

Six weeks had elapsed since she had come home to Willow Creek Ranch. Six weeks spent lying, conniving, and manipulating. Six weeks of dodging guilt and battling fear of being found out. Six of the most miserable weeks of her life.

Oh, she was contented enough with her day-to-day. Chasing after Buster and Angel kept her occupied. She fed them, bathed them, dressed them. She read stories and took them on pony rides. She slipped into her bathing suit and splashed with the children in the lawn sprinkler. She braided Angel's hair and fussed over Buster when he made a fist, flexed his biceps, and proudly showed her his "muscles."

But mentally, emotionally, she was a wreck.

Coming home had not brought the peace of mind she assumed it would bring. No matter how hard she tried, Deannie could not stop thinking about Brodie. She saw him around the ranch as he did his chores and joined them for meals. He was pleasant and didn't avoid conversation with her, but he kept things light and polite and made sure they were never alone together.

He'd burrowed under her skin but good, and the thought of when he found out about her deception, he'd feel so betrayed sat like an anchor on her shoulders. He trusted her when he shouldn't. He'd opened his home to her. He'd given her a job and treated her as if she were family.

She'd gone to the cabin once to check on Kenny's progress, but he'd told her it was best if she stayed away and let Kenny heal in his own time.

With each passing day, tension mounted as Deannie struggled with her internal turmoil.

It reminded Deannie of that old musical *Seven Brides for Seven Brothers* where the naughty menfolk were banished to the barn for the winter. It felt like that, so close to Brodie, and yet, so far. She and Emma living in the big rambling farmhouse with the kids, with Kenny and Brodie isolated in the log cabin, miles from the ranch's main hub. Even though Emma had no idea what was going on.

"Quarter for your thoughts." Emma's voice shook her out of her worrying that early July afternoon.

"Huh?"

Deannie looked up from where they sat shelling peas at the kitchen table. The smell of brisket in the smoker on the back patio wafted in through the open window. The baby was sleeping in his bassinet beside them. Angel and Buster sat on the floor making Fourth of July decorations for the upcoming holiday with construction paper, glitter, and paste.

"You've been so far away lately," Emma prodded. "Is there anything you'd like to talk about?"

"No," Deannie murmured.

"I wish Kenny would call," Emma fretted. "I can't believe he hasn't even come by to see the baby."

"Maybe he found a job out of town," Deannie said.

"Not very likely. He's probably living at the Lonesome Dove. Deannie, I know Kenny has his faults, but I always thought he loved me and the kids." Emma sniffled.

"Don't give up hope." She leaned over to pat Emma's hand. "Maybe your ultimatum woke him up. Anyone can change if they want it badly enough."

"If that's true, then where is he?" Emma pressed the hem of her shirt against her eyes to stay the tears.

"Maybe he went to rehab?"

"On what? We're broke."

Deannie glanced out the window and spied Brodie striding up the walk. Joy leaped in her heart. Oh! He was so handsome with his straw Stetson clutched in his hands. Her arms ached to hold him; her lips longed to kiss him.

He knocked at the back door before opening it. "Hi!" He greeted everyone with a wide smile, but his gaze slid over Deannie. He lowered his voice, met her eyes directly, and repeated, "Hi."

"Hey," she whispered.

"Hello, stranger," Emma said. "Whatcha been up to?"

"Getting that cabin straightened up."

"When are you going to move back in here?" Emma asked. "It's plumb ridiculous you hiding out in that cabin just because I had a baby. Phillip is only waking up once a night now."

"Maybe soon." He exchanged glances with Deannie, then quickly looked away.

"Any word from Kenny?" Emma asked, rolling her hands into fists.

"Actually, that's what I came in to tell you."

Emma's face paled, and she laid a hand over her heart. "Is anything wrong? Kenny's not hurt, is he?"

"Kenny's fine, but he'd like permission to spend the holiday with you and the kids."

"Since when did Kenny Trueblood ever need my permission to do anything?"

"Since now."

Everyone looked over to see Kenny standing on the porch, looking humbled.

"Daddy!" Buster and Angel cried in unison.

"Kenny?" Emma rose to her feet, her palm pressed flat against her throat.

"Hello, Emma," Kenny said, his voice thick with emotion. He let himself in through the back door and scooped up a child in each arm. He kissed his children on the tops of their heads, all the while keeping his eyes trained on his wife's face.

Something inside Deannie cracked. Another chunk of her defenses broke right off, leaving her vulnerable. How had she gotten so involved in the daily lives of these people? She'd never meant to fall in love with all of them, but she had. For fifteen years, her goal had stayed prominent in her mind—win back Willow Creek.

But she'd discovered things were simply not that easy. From the very beginning, when she had stepped into the Lonesome Dove and discovered Rafe Trueblood was dead, her plans had unraveled, forcing Deannie to question her goals and reexamine her motives. Was recovering her home worth hurting the people she cared about so deeply? How much was she willing to sacrifice for revenge, and what price was too high to pay?

Deannie watched the scene unfolding between husband and wife, her fingers laced together, her back stiff with tension.

"Where have you been?" Emma asked Kenny, her whole body trembling.

"Living in the cabin with Brodie."

"Why didn't you come to see us? We have a new baby!

"I was afraid you didn't want me around." Kenny hung his head. "I have been little of a husband lately."

"We worried about you."

"I got something to tell you, Emma." Tears misted Kenny's eyes.

"Yes?" She clutched her hands and stepped toward him. They had eyes only for each other.

"I've been so wrong."

"What are you saying?"

"Brodie's helped me realize it."

"Deannie's been talking to me, too. I'd forgotten how blessed I am to have a family." Emma smiled gratefully at her.

"Honey, you were one hundred percent in the right. You've done nothing wrong."

"That's not true, Kenny. I nagged, I harangued, I made you feel like less of a man."

"If you hadn't threatened divorce, I might never have straightened up my act, but I swear to you I haven't touched a drop of liquor in six weeks. I've been going to AA meetings. Brodie's been my sober companion. I got a job working for Hubert Barnes at the feed store. It's not much, but it's a start."

"Oh, Kenny," Emma said.

He raised a palm. "Let me finish. Brodie wants to give us our half of the ranch. We can build our home on the back acreage. He will also give us a hundred head of cattle to start our own herd."

"Is it true?" she whispered. "Did you really give up your bad habits for me and the kids?"

"Absolutely, sweetheart. You are the light of my life. Can you ever forgive me?" Kenny dropped to his knees and reached out for his wife. "I love you, Emma. I always have, and I always will."

"I love you, too, Kenny. From the moment you came driving up to my dorm room at Texas Tech on that bad-boy motorcycle of yours." Emma sobbed and dissolved into her husband's waiting arms.

No matter what problems Emma and Kenny faced, their love for each other was clear in their voices, the way they held each other, the lingering looks they exchanged.

But none of it would have happened without Brodie pushing his brother to change.

Deannie's heart swelled in her chest. Would anyone ever love her like that? Was there a man who could forgive all her faults and overlook her sins? She cast a glance at Brodie, and her breath snagged.

He was studying her intently. His dark eyes narrowed and grew shiny against the sunlight flooding in through the window.

They locked gazes, and time seemed suspended.

She would never forget this moment. It would hang in her brain whenever she conjured up images of the Fourth of July. No longer would firecrackers and barbecue and watermelon dominate her memories of Independence Day. Instead, Deanna Rene Hollis would always remember the date as the exact instant when she realized she had fallen head over heels in love with Brodie Trueblood.

STARING INTO DEANNIE'S EYES, BRODIE FELT AS IF he'd finally found what he'd been searching for his entire life—someone to love. Perhaps it was emotions caused by Kenny and Emma's tearful reunion, but that didn't change the feelings whipping and diving inside him as Deannie's gaze merged with his in a head-on collision of the heart.

"I better go check the brisket," Deannie said, clearing her throat and breaking their connection.

Emma and Kenny, still locked in their embrace, were oblivious.

"How 'bout me and the kids giving you a hand," Brodie offered, wanting to give his brother time alone with his wife. Truthfully, he was just as eager to be alone with Deannie, but that wasn't about to happen with Buster and Angel clinging to his hands.

"Come on, troops," Deannie sang out, picking up a pot holder and a pair of tongs on her way through the kitchen.

He picked up the kids and followed her outside, his

gaze riveted to Deannie's backside. Her thick red mane swished below her shoulders, causing a riot inside him.

Brodie gulped. Six weeks without her had been too long.

Sure, he'd seen her. He'd watched her as she went about her daily chores. He'd talked to her over meals with the other hands. But it had been six long weeks since he'd been within touching distance. His fingers ached to skim her soft skin; his lips hungered to taste her sweet mouth; his nose twitched to burrow against that long, pale neck and inhale her glorious magnolia scent.

"Why don't you kids go play?" Brodie sat them down and pointed to the swing set. "While I help Aunt Deannie with the food."

Aunt Deannie.

Where had that come from?

She hadn't missed the slip of his tongue. She smiled and ducked her head, her cheeks pinking with pleasure. She lifted the lid on the smoker, giving him a potent dose of cooking brisket. Brodie's mouth watered, but not from the want of food.

"That was really wonderful what you did for Kenny and Emma," she said, studiously flipping the meat.

"Kenny's my brother. Nothing makes me happier than peace in the family at last. We talked it through and both realized my father is the one who kept our rivalry stirred up."

"Oh?"

"We got a lot of hard feelings out of the way."

"That's nice," she murmured.

"Also, out there in the cabin, I had a lot of time to think."

"What about?"

Darn it, he wished she would look at him. "*Us.*"

"Us?" she echoed.

Was that fear he heard in her voice? Tentatively, he reached over and touched her shoulder.

She kept her lashes lowered and didn't look at him again.

"You know," he said hoarsely. "Us. As in you and me."

"Brodie...I..."

"I know I said we'd wait three months before we discussed changing our relationship, but these past six weeks without you have been pure torture. I missed you, Deannie, more than you can know."

Please, he thought, *please let her give us a chance.*

But she said nothing. Just waited with the tongs outstretched in her hand.

"Look at me."

Her lashes fluttered and she gulped. Briefly her eyes met his, but then she quickly glanced away again as if desperately hiding something. "I thought you had a lot of reservations about me."

"I'm not saying we should jump into anything. I just wanted you to know I'm moving back into the house."

"Thanks for telling me." She pulled back. "Gotta get supper on the table."

Reluctantly, he let her go, confused. Did she want to be with him or not? The woman sent mixed messages, and he simply did not know how to read her.

Brodie swallowed hard and realized it didn't matter. Whatever secrets she harbored were hers to keep. He would back off for now, give her the time and space she needed to come to him. They could work things out. For he was a patient man.

14

I t was the Fourth of July, and Deannie hadn't gotten a wink of sleep. She'd lain awake all night thinking of Brodie. The day had been busy with activities, but now, after dark, they sat outside waiting for the fireworks display to begin.

One thought circled her mind. She had to leave Willow Creek. As soon as possible. Get out of here before Brodie did what she'd been angling for him to do ever since she'd faked a broken-down car—ask her to marry him.

Because once he uttered those four little words, it would be all over.

Looking over her shoulder, she studied his profile in the gathering twilight, and her heart jerked. He was so handsome, so kind, so honest.

If only she'd known! She would never have started down this road. Her dark motives had repercussions beyond her control. Repercussions that could cause many people pain. In that respect, she did not differ

from Rafe, putting her own agenda ahead of everything and everyone.

Sorrow was her penance, losing both Willow Creek and Brodie's love. Sadness, remorse, and regret melded into a tight ball in her throat. She'd made so many bad decisions. The honorable choice was to disappear from his life forever and spend the rest of *her* life trying to be a better person.

They were on the back porch in twin rocking chairs enjoying the lazy evening heat. Hummingbirds hovered near the feeder, drinking one last time before settling down for the night. The grass was damp from the sprinklers.

After a hearty supper of sliced barbecue, potato salad, baked beans, corn on the cob, and homemade peach ice cream, Kenny and Emma had taken the baby and disappeared upstairs arm in arm, leaving the other two children with Deannie and Brodie.

Angel sat in Deannie's lap, Buster in Brodie's. They had already had their baths and dressed in pajamas. Cooter Gates joined them, and he leisurely gnawed on the stem of an unlit pipe while they waited for Rory and the other ranch hands to start the fireworks just beyond the chain-link fence.

Stars lit the edge of the sky as the sun slipped behind the horizon. Crickets chirped. Cattle lowed. Honeysuckle drifted on the air and mingled with the scent of charcoal.

Tears nudged against the back of Deannie's eyes. Angel leaned into her chest, and Deannie lightly kissed the top of her head. The child smelled of bubble bath and strawberry shampoo.

She would leave tonight after the kids were in bed, Deannie decided. It was the only way.

"You folks ready?" Rory hollered from across the fence.

"Yes!" Angel and Buster squealed in unison.

Brodie chuckled. The happy sound filled Deannie's ears, twisting her already-raw emotions like the tightening of a screw.

Torture.

Sitting here in the pleasant evening, expecting fireworks, children clutched in their laps, they were the epitome of an ordinary couple on the Fourth of July. The illusion tormented her. Deep inside, this was what Deannie had longed her whole life to recover. Willow Creek. An intact family unit. An honorable man to love her.

Closing her eyes, she swallowed past her grief.

Her goal was within reach; all she had to do was take it, but the victory was hollow. She couldn't accept it. She'd manipulated and finagled. She'd lied and deceived. Once Brodie knew the truth, he would no longer love her.

Yes, everything she'd ever wanted was within her grasp, but she could not close her fist and take it.

The sudden explosion startled her.

She jumped, jostling Angel into her chin, and Deannie's eyes flew open just as the rocket flared into a starburst of bright colors.

"Wow," Buster exclaimed and clapped his hands.

The gunpowder odor, thick and metallic, invaded their nostrils. Rory torched another wick, and the second rocket followed the first.

"Ah," Cooter Gates exclaimed. "I love the smell of the Fourth of July. It's nice having kids at the ranch again."

Deannie lightly caressed Angel's bare arm and strained to hear Cooter, who spoke softly and was sitting on the other side of Brodie.

Cooter stared unseeingly into the past, his pipe cupped in his palm. "Yep," he whispered. "I can still remember Gil Hollis's little girl laughing and squealing when I was the one setting off the fireworks."

Deannie froze, her heart thumping in her chest. Did Cooter suspect?

"I've got a headache," Deannie said, rubbing her temple. It wasn't a lie. "Could you put the children to bed?"

"You okay?" Brodie patted her hand.

The tenderness in his eyes, the concern in his voice had her stomach rolling over. She did not deserve his kindness.

"I just need to lie down for a while."

"Sure, sure. Go on upstairs," Brodie assured her. "Come on, Angel, get in my lap."

Deannie transferred the girl to the crook of his arm and almost ran into the house, desperate to escape. She fled to her room, the tears she'd pushed back for so long streaming down her cheeks.

Dropping to her knees, she dragged her duffel bag from under the bed, then began emptying out the dresser drawers and stuffing her things inside. She had to go. It would be far too easy to stay, to pretend she'd never had revenge on her mind. To let herself fall completely in love with Brodie. To marry him, raise his children, stay with him for the rest of her life, and carry her secret to her grave.

But how could she do such a thing? How could they ever build a life together with no real trust between them? How could she spend a lifetime deceiving the man she cared about more than anything? More even than Willow Creek Ranch.

Packed and ready, she lay on the bed fully dressed and waited.

An hour passed.

Outside, the fireworks continued. She heard the resounding bangs, the sizzles and pops. She saw the colored lights flare and dissipate through the thin lace curtains of her bedroom window. She smelled gunpowder and barbecue smoke lingering on her skin and in her hair.

Deannie groaned and covered her head with the pillow, trying her best to shut out everything.

At long last, the noises stopped. She strained for the sounds of Brodie trooping up the stairs. She heard his boots against the wood and his murmured voice as he tucked the children into their beds. Then she heard him moving outside her door.

She squeezed her eyes shut and held her breath.

The door creaked open slightly. She could feel him standing in the doorway staring at her.

"Good night, Deannie," he whispered, then pulled the door closed behind him.

She stayed another hour, listening to the old house settle. Finally, convinced everyone was asleep, she slid off the bed, gathered her duffel, took a deep breath, and edged from the room.

Night-lights lit the hallway. All the bedroom doors were closed. Satisfied she was alone, Deannie eased downstairs.

A floorboard creaked, and she caught her breath. Her pulse roared louder than an idling race car engine. The trip through the quiet house seemed to take an eternity, her memory snagging at each step.

Here, on the stairs, was where she'd tripped and fallen, and Brodie caught her in his arms.

There, in the living room, was where she had sat with Emma, holding the baby and listening to her friend's troubles.

In the kitchen by the stove was where she had cooked for the ranch hands.

And the dining room was where she and Brodie had shared their first meal together. She could taste the roast beef sandwiches he'd made.

Fresh tears scorched her cheeks by the time she reached the back door. How she wanted to stay! To leave her sad past behind and embrace the future. But to do so would mean living a lie, and she simply could not go through with it.

Locking the back door behind her, she stepped out into the warm night air, her car keys clutched firmly in her hand. A half-moon hung in the sky, lighting her way across the drive.

She kept her head down, too heartbroken to look back.

"Deannie." His voice snaked out of the darkness and wrapped around her.

Brodie.

His boots crunched on the gravel. She didn't have to

turn to know he had been sitting in the shadows on the front porch and was now standing behind her.

"Where are you going?" Brodie asked, the confusion in his voice impossible to miss. "You were sneaking off in the middle of the night without saying goodbye?"

She stood like a statue, unable to move, unable to answer.

"Deannie." His hand closed over her upper arm, and he turned her to face him.

She met his somber gaze, and all resistance left her body. How could she leave this man? She did not deserve him, but how she wanted him!

"Brodie...I..."

"Where were you going?" he repeated, his dark eyes shimmering with unexpressed emotion.

"It's for the best," she said.

His grip tightened. "What are you talking about? We've got something going on here, you and me. I tried to deny it at first, but my feelings for you won't go away. I stopped fighting it and let things happen naturally."

Deannie whistled in a breath. "I can't do this."

"I know you're scared. I know there's something from your past that's keeping you on the run, but please, Deannie, don't shut me out. Give us a chance to work through it."

How tempting it would be to accept his generous offer! To fling herself into his arms and confess everything. But once he discovered the truth, that she had planned and schemed her way onto the ranch, the love shinning in his eyes would wither and die.

"You don't understand," she said.

"I think I do." His fingers rubbed her skin in a

smoothing circle. "I get it. You need more from me than empty promises of what might one day be. You need a commitment."

"Oh, Brodie." She opened her mouth to tell him no, to beg him not to say what was on his mind, but it was too late.

Brodie took a deep breath and spoke the words that Deannie had been waiting to hear from the moment she stepped into his headlights on the roadside. The words that would offer her everything she'd ever wanted. The words she had no willpower to reject.

"I love you, Deannie McCellan, and I want to marry you."

And then Deannie said, "Yes," because she loved him too.

BRODIE WAITED AT THE ALTAR. HE WORE SHARPLY creased black denim jeans and brand new black boots under a black tuxedo jacket and white shirt. The stiff collar closed tighter around his throat, cutting off his oxygen supply.

The pianist had played the wedding march three times. The guests were shifting in their seats, craning their necks and staring expectantly at the staircase.

Kenny, appearing nervous and uncomfortable, waited beside him. At the back of the room, Angel nibbled on a white rose petal plucked from her wicker basket, and Buster, a white satin pillow clutched between his fists, wriggled impatiently.

The minister, Bible open in his palms, cleared his throat and raised his eyebrows.

Brodie shot a look at Emma. She shrugged and telegraphed him a helpless expression.

Deannie will stand me up. The thought flashed through his mind and sent a spiked stab angling through his gut. No. Not that. Anything but that.

A hush settled over the small crowd. The clock over the mantel ticked loudly, expectantly. Brodie felt the blood drain from his body. The room grew suddenly boiling as every eye in the place rested upon him.

"Perhaps," the minister whispered, "you should go check on the bride."

Nodding, Brodie moved as if on automatic pilot. He turned, walked past his family and friends, and marched up the stairs. Without even looking, he knew what he would find when he reached the bedroom he and Deannie were supposed to share as man and wife.

Still, the reality of that empty room slammed him like a sucker punch to the solar plexus.

The window hung open; the screen was missing, and the curtain flapped in the breeze. The room smelled of her perfume. Like a fragrant magnolia in full bloom, but she was nowhere in sight.

"Deannie?" Brodie said, even though he knew there would be no sweet reply.

Why?

That word reverberated in his brain, and he had no answer. *Why, Deannie, why?*

He stepped to the window and stared out at the cars below. Her battered old sedan sat hemmed in by visitors' vehicles. If she'd run, she'd done it on foot.

His stomach burned; his chest squeezed; his pulse turned as thready as an unspooling ribbon.

No.

He trod the carpet, pacing, fighting the fog enveloping his mind. His boot connected with something.

An earring.

Tiny, white, delicate.

Brodie dropped to his knees, scooped up the earring, and cupped it in his hands. It looked so incongruous, that petite white pearl contrasting with his large callused palms.

He almost broke down at that moment. The hollow ache deep inside his soul that had started as a boy when he could never win his father's affections widened into a yawning chasm. In Deannie, he'd thought he'd found what he'd lost with his mother's death—someone to love him, truly, honestly, unconditionally.

What did her departure mean? Had she gotten cold feet? Was she scared of marriage and commitment? Or had his greatest fear come to pass—she'd never really loved him to begin with.

Crouching beside the open window, Brodie ran a hand through his hair and tried to think. There had to be an explanation. Deannie wouldn't change her mind so quickly without a damned good reason.

But what?

He recalled that night he'd asked her to be his bride. The memory rose bittersweet and prophetic in his mind. He should have known something was very wrong, something that lurked deep within her psyche. She had been trying to leave him even then.

When he'd spied her sneaking out to her car, duffel bag in her hand, his spirits had sunk to his feet. Without thinking, without planning, without rehearsing his words, he'd intercepted Deannie.

She had accepted his proposal willingly, throwing herself into his arms with unbridled emotion. At that moment, any doubts he'd harbored about their relationship had vanished. He no longer feared that she wanted him just for his ranch and his money. When he'd crushed her to his chest, felt her heart beating against his, he hadn't faltered. Asking her to marry him had come as easily as breathing.

And the ensuing weeks before the wedding had been pure heaven. They'd been so close. Laughing, talking, sharing, spending every free moment together. The single area that caused him concern was Deannie's continued reluctance to discuss her past. Every time he mentioned his childhood and encouraged her to open up about hers, she skirted the issue by changing the subject or giving him one-word replies. Since then she'd otherwise been cheerful and bubbly, and he'd dropped the issue, but now he realized he should have pushed.

"Brodie?" Kenny stood in the doorway, his hands clasped. "Are you okay, little brother?"

"She's gone," Brodie replied, the hard little pearl earring cold in his fist. "Deannie ran out on me."

Kenny walked over and clapped a hand on his shoulder. "I'm sorry."

Brodie swallowed hard. "The hell of it is, I don't even know why she stood me up. I thought we were so happy. These past few months have been paradise. We never fought. We got along great. I guess I should have known it was too good to be true."

"I don't know what to say."

"I've got to find her." Brodie rose to his feet. "She couldn't have gotten far. Her car's still here."

"What about your truck?"

Brodie peered out the window and spotted his pickup parked under the carport where he'd left it. "No. There's the truck."

"You think she just took off walking?"

"I don't know what to think. Maybe she's hiding right here in the house, waiting for everyone to leave."

"Nah," Kenny went to the window. "Screen's on the ground; there are bootprints in the dirt. Deannie jumped out this window."

The image wrenched—Deannie, so desperate to get away from him she would leap from a second-story bedroom in her wedding gown.

"Hey, didn't I see Ranger saddled in the corral earlier?"

Brodie nodded. "Could be. Rory took him out to exercise him."

"Well, I hate to alarm you, but he's gone."

Just like Deannie.

"You think she left on the horse?" Brodie asked his brother.

"Yep."

"What's going on?" Emma appeared in the doorway. "The crowd's getting restless. Where's Deannie?"

"Gone," Brodie said sadly.

Emma frowned and tapped the face of her watch. "I

talked to her not fifteen minutes ago. Where could she be?"

Brodie pivoted on his heels to face his sister-in-law. "How did she act? What did she say?"

"She acted nervous, like all brides. I tried to reassure her," Emma said. "I told her love was worth all the ups and downs."

She looked at her husband with adoring eyes. Kenny walked over and slipped his arm around her waist.

"I've got to find her," Brodie said.

Brodie was halfway down the stairs before he remembered he had a roomful of guests assembled. All eyes turned his way. Brodie took a deep breath. He didn't have time for them. He had to find Deannie and sort this out.

Through a blur, Brodie surveyed his friends and family. Angel was curled up in one corner, fast asleep, her thumb in her mouth. Buster had undone his tie and was busily working on his shoes. The minister had taken a seat and was leafing through the Bible. The ranch hands focused industriously on the carpet.

Obviously, his face gave him away, for the crowd immediately broke into a speculative hum the minute they saw him. Just as Brodie opened his mouth to tell everyone to go home, the front door swung inward, and Matilda Jennings burst across the threshold, her iron-gray hair in wild disarray, a sheaf of papers clutched in her hand.

"Stop the wedding!" his former housekeeper shouted. "I have proof the bride's a fraud!"

Deannie rode like hellhounds were snarling at her heels. Ranger galloped across the rough terrain, his hooves skimming over rocks and cactus and tumbleweed. Deannie crouched low in the saddle, her train billowing behind her, pristine as a sail.

It's over.

The tenderness, the compassion, the understanding that had begun as a ruse but quickly turned to love, lost to her forever. She had deceived Brodie in the worst way possible. Then, because she was a coward, as surely as her father had been when he'd faced Rafe Trueblood that awful night so long ago, she'd compounded it by accepting his proposal and planning a wedding.

By leaving Brodie at the altar, Deannie had humiliated him in front of his friends and family. How much kinder it would have been to refuse him on the Fourth of July when he'd proposed, instead of letting herself float along on a river of denial.

She had told herself that everything would be all

right. That their love could conquer anything. Anything except marrying him under false pretenses.

Brodie deserved someone who would love him freely, unconditionally, with no ulterior motives. For, deep inside her soul, Deannie couldn't say for sure if she'd fallen in love with Brodie the man, or Brodie, owner of Willow Creek Ranch.

A hundred different miseries washed over her in unrelenting waves. Deannie swallowed back salty tears. Her nose was stuffed up, and she knew her eyes were red and puffy from crying and riding into the arid wind.

She hadn't consciously headed for the log cabin, her heart magnetized by the past. Some part of her was still looking for answers, still hoping to discover who she really was.

Ranger was breathing hard as she slowed him to a trot and scaled the creek bed. Twilight shadows pushed the sun from the sky, and it was pitch-black by the time Deannie wheeled the horse into the yard.

Confused and hurting, she tumbled down off the gelding's back and headed for the small sanctuary. Here, she could rest and inspect her life. Since her thirst for revenge had evaporated and she would never own Willow Creek, she needed to find a new purpose for being. Preferably an unselfish purpose that would make up for her grievous errors.

Fumbling with the knob, Deannie finally ripped the door open and staggered inside, her vision blinded by tears. She flicked on the lights and, blinking, glanced around the room.

It was a far cry from the disheveled mess that had greeted her the day she and Brodie had cleaned the cabin together. The memory of that day, not so very long ago, snared in her imagination and refused to leave.

She could see him as vividly as if he were standing before her now, looking sumptuous in those fire-engine red briefs. The contours of his well-proportioned fanny coaxing her, the outline of his broad shoulders enticing her, his rugged outdoorsy scent wrapping around her senses and refusing to let go.

"Brodie." Deannie gulped and closed her eyes, willing away the erotic vision. How long before she forgot the taste of his mouth, the feel of his skin, the sound of his voice, low, deep, and tender?

Opening her eyes, she listlessly wandered through the house, taking in the changes. The bedrooms were immaculately clean and neatly organized. Odds and ends had been stored in boxes and their contents clearly labeled. Books. Material. Christmas decorations. Dishes. Linens. Mama's personal things. Rafe's papers.

Deannie's fingers lingered over that box, and she sucked in her breath, surprised to shake at the thought of thumbing through the personal papers of the man she hated.

Not really knowing why, she lifted the box from the stack and carried it over to the bed. Pushing her bridal veil from her face, she settled down on the covers and removed the box lid.

The contents smelled of cigar smoke and whiskey. Deannie crinkled her nose, and a sudden jolt of sadness knifed through her. She and Brodie had so much in common. Both with fathers who'd taken the wrong paths in life, both afraid to trust, to let down their guards, both seeking security and stability in the land that meant so much to them.

Deannie leafed through the papers. Doctor bills, bank statements, a lavender-scented birthday card signed "All my love, Melinda." She kept digging, not really sure why she was looking.

A final notice from a collection agency postmarked the year Rafe had won the ranch from Gil, a faded photograph of Willow Creek taken from the road, and a letter addressed to her father but never mailed.

Deannie's hands trembled so furiously she dropped the letter, and it sailed to the floor. Bending over, she reclaimed it and ripped open the sealed envelope. Dated three weeks before her father had killed himself.

Dear Gil,

I got a confession to make. I ain't proud of what I did, but I did it for a good reason. I don't know if you'll understand, and I'm damned sure you won't forgive me, but I got to clear my conscience and tell you what's on my mind. I'm dying and I want to set the record straight. Remember that night you lost Willow Creek? Hell, what am I saying? How could you forget losing your home? Well, truth is, I cheated. I pulled that ace of spades out of my sleeve. I was desperate, and desperate men do desperate things. See, I was about to go to jail for writing hot checks to feed my family. The judge told me if I could prove I had a permanent residence and gainful employment, then he'd give me probation. Plus, Melinda was fixing to leave me. She'd finally had enough of living in shacks and puttin' up with my bad habits. I know it's no excuse.

I put you and your girl on the street to cover my tail. I'm sorry for it now and wish to hell I hadn't done it, but I did. I got some money, and I'd like to send you a little. It won't make up for nothing, but maybe your girl can use it to go to college or something.

The letter was signed simply, Rafe Trueblood.

Enclosed was a cashier's check for twenty-five thousand dollars.

Deannie stared at the letter as the words sank in. In the last months of his life, Rafe Trueblood had been seeking forgiveness. And yet, he hadn't mailed it. Why not? Had he heard about her father's suicide and decided his debt was paid?

A well-worn deck of playing cards with a rubber band wrapped around it lay at the bottom of the box, and Deannie just *knew* those were the cards Rafe had used to steal Willow Creek from her father.

In that instant, all her old anger came rushing back. It oozed through her, hot and vicious, as she tasted raw bitterness. She picked up the cards and hurled them against the wall.

Panting, she kicked at the bed and howled her rage. She howled for her missing childhood, for the home she'd given up, for the father who'd slipped away from her forever.

But most of all, she howled over losing Brodie.

Deannie gritted her teeth in agony and twisted the skirt of her wedding gown in her fists; she heard the material rip, but she no longer cared.

How dare Rafe Trueblood steal everything from her! If he hadn't already been dead, she could have strangled him with her bare hands in that black moment. How many lives had that awful man destroyed? His wife's, her father's, Brodie's. Her own.

"Rafe Trueblood, you lying, conniving, thieving, cheating, son of a..." she swore.

Her chest heaved. Her breath whistled in through her teeth. Her body shuddered. Hatred, that comfortable old emotion, boiled up inside Deannie, embracing her like a friend.

No! A part of her shouted. The part of her that over the past few months had learned to let go of hatred and replace it with love.

Then just as quickly as it came, her anger disappeared, dissipating in the aftermath of her adrenaline surge. What was the point? Getting mad would change nothing. Seeking revenge had only made things worse. For the first time in fifteen years, Deanna Rene Hollis saw the past with clear, unbiased eyes.

All this time wasted holding a grudge. Yes, she'd suffered a great injustice. Yes, life wasn't fair. But retaliation solved nothing. It only lowered her to Rafe's level. Did she want to end up like the gambler, old and sick, alienated from his family, ostracized by his community, reaching out in the last days of his life with no one to heed his pathetic pleas for forgiveness?

Even if Rafe had cheated, her father had been as much to blame. No one had forced him to drink; no one had held a gun to his head and told him to gamble his homestead on the turn of a card game.

All these years she'd been seeking a monster to hold accountable for her woes. Rafe had not been a good person, but he was only human. Sure, his motives were shady, but the man had his reasons for his behavior. Beneath that bravado, hidden by booze and a glib attitude, had lurked a sad, lonely man unable to live up to his responsibilities.

Holding on to hate would not bring her father back. It would not erase the pain she had suffered, nor would it absolve her of the hurt she'd caused Brodie. She'd been wrong to hold him accountable for his father's actions. He was no more answerable for Rafe than she'd been for Gil.

She would forgive Rafe for what he had done those many years ago, all the while hoping and praying that someday Brodie could find it in his heart to forgive her for lying to him and leaving him standing alone at the altar. It was the only thing that gave Deannie any comfort. The only thing she had to hold on to.

❧

"DEANNIE MCCELLAN, YOUR WIFE-TO-BE..." MATILDA cackled maliciously, "...is none other than the daughter of Gilbert Hollis, the man from whom your father won Willow Creek in a poker game."

A collective gasp went up from the crowd. Brodie frowned, absorbing the implication of the woman's words.

Cooter Gates rose to his feet, his eyes staring unseeingly. "Little Deannie's come home?" he whispered. "I thought her voice sounded familiar, but I figured my old ears were playing tricks on me!"

"You bet!" Matilda gleefully shook the paper under Brodie's nose. "This is a copy of her birth certificate and driver's license. Her real name is Deanna Rene Hollis, and she's marrying you simply to get her hands on this ranch."

"You're wrong," Brodie said, his voice cracking like a whip. "Deannie just stood me up at the altar, so obviously that's not true." He opened his arms wide and made shooing motions. "Show's over, folks. Everyone can go home."

With that, he turned on his heels and stalked out of the house still wearing his tuxedo, his mind struggling to process Matilda's jarring revelation.

Deannie was the daughter of Gil Hollis, previous owner of Willow Creek Ranch? The man his father had swindled?

Brodie's ego deflated like a tire going flat. He'd allowed himself to fall in love, only to discover Deannie was living a lie.

She'd come back to Willow Creek to reclaim her heritage. That was the truth of it. She didn't love him. She never had. It had all been a charade—her kisses, her hugs, her sweet declarations of love, a well-orchestrated act and nothing more.

Wincing, Brodie rubbed his throbbing temple. Suddenly everything made perfect sense. Deannie had been at the Lonesome Dove gambling with Kenny hoping to win back the ranch the same way her daddy had lost it. Apparently, in the course of the poker game, she'd discovered Brodie had inherited Willow Creek, not his older brother.

A dizzy sensation rocked his head. Brodie could see Deannie deciding to come after him. Finding out he wasn't a gambling man had probably put a kink in her plans. But Deannie was cunning. She was resourceful.

She zeroed in on his weakness. She'd taken advantage of his need for love, his desire for a family, and she'd schemed her way into his heart.

She must have faked car problems to weasel her way onto Willow Creek. Then Lady Luck had been in her corner when he'd fired Matilda. He'd been so easy to manipulate. Putty in the hands of a true professional.

He swallowed against the memory. He'd played right into her wily plot, practically begging her to help him with the kids until Emma came home from the hospital. And she'd wasted no time making herself indispensable.

Deannie was some kind of actress, he had to give her credit. When she had kissed him, he'd felt sparks beyond imagination which now made his blood run cold. The woman was more heartless and underhanded than Rafe had ever been.

Wadding his hands into fists, Brodie rode the wave of betrayal washing through him. Like a helpless buoy on storm-crazed seas, his emotions lashed at him, hard and relentless.

Dunce. Dupe. Sucker.

In his desperate search for love, he'd brought this sorrow upon his own head. He should have checked Deannie's background before hiring her as his house-keeper. He should have asked questions when Rory had discovered nothing amiss with her car. He should have listened to that niggling voice in the back of his mind that urged him not to get involved with her.

Instead, he'd been a fool for love.

Just like his mother, letting his heart rule his head. Caring about someone who did not love him in return.

Guests filtered from the house behind him, talking

in hushed tones, but Brodie's personal pain was so great he didn't even notice as they climbed into their vehicles and drove away.

Clutching the corral fence in both hands, he stared across the pasture at the craggy landscape that meant so much to him. The sun was slipping low beyond the horizon, orange and purple fingers of light reaching for one last grasp before nightfall.

He studied the tall yellow grass, the short mesquite trees, the mass of cacti. It wasn't the prettiest place in the world, but it was the only real home he'd ever known. It was also the land that Deannie had wanted back so badly that she'd been willing to marry a man she did not love to get it.

But she hadn't gone through with the marriage. At the last minute, Deannie had run away.

Why?

Could it be that she loved him and therefore couldn't say "I do" under false pretenses? A glimmer of hope flared in his chest, but Brodie didn't dare fan that faint ember.

"Brodie!"

Kenny's shout brought his head up. Brodie turned to see his brother striding toward him.

"Ranger's back."

Brodie's eyes met Kenny's. "And Deannie?"

His brother shook his head. "No sign of her, but Ranger was dragging the saddle behind him."

Anxiety coiled through Brodie's gut. "You think she fell off?"

Kenny shrugged. "Is she a good rider?"

"I don't know," Brodie replied. There were so many

things he didn't know about her. He'd assumed his love for her was enough, that it could conquer anything. He'd been so wrong.

"You going to look for her?"

Brodie nodded grimly. He had no choice. It didn't matter whether she loved him. He loved her, cared about her, wanted nothing bad to happen to her. He couldn't leave her out there alone in the dark not knowing if she was hurt or scared or lonely.

His gut torqued at the thought she could be injured. When he got down to it, her safety meant much more than anything.

"Will you put Ranger up for me, Kenny? I'll take the truck and drive the land."

"Okay." His brother stepped closer. "For what it's worth, I hope you and Deannie work things out. If anybody was made for each other, you two are."

Shrugging off his brother's comment, Brodie headed for the pickup with *Just Married* in shoe polish on the windows. He climbed inside the cab and roared from the driveway, tin cans clanking noisily from the bumper.

The sound mocked him, reminding him of what he'd lost this day. With the heel of one palm, Brodie pushed his hair off his forehead and stared grimly through the shoe-polished windshield. He flicked on the headlights, his gaze glued to the swath that sliced through the darkness.

Please let her be all right, he prayed. What would he do if he found her? Brodie clenched his jaw as a worse thought occurred to him. What if he didn't find her? She'd be gone, and he'd never know for sure the reason she'd jumped from the second-story window and left him standing at the altar like a fool.

He trod on the accelerator and followed the fence row, his stomach bumping and grinding along with the truck.

Without even thinking, he turned the truck in the cabin's direction. Conflicting thoughts ping-ponged in his head, volleying back and forth as he mentally reviewed everything that had happened.

Deannie loves me; she loves me not. His mind vacillated between those two painful alternatives.

Ten minutes later, the pickup crested the rise, and Brodie stared down into the valley where the log cabin crouched beside the creek bed, flanked on either side by an abundance of willow trees.

A lone light shone from the small house, and his heart took wings.

Deannie. It had to be her.

He stopped the truck and killed the engine. He didn't want to pull into the driveway and spook her into running. He had to see her, had to speak to her, had to wring an explanation from her.

Shutting the pickup's door quietly, he walked the few yards to the house, his pulse pounding louder, more insistently with each step.

He hesitated on the front porch, his gaze riveted by what he saw through the window.

Deannie sat on the sofa, an old photograph album in her lap. She still wore her western-cut wedding gown. The one they'd special-ordered.

A lump blocked his throat as he watched her press a tissue to her eyes. She was crying. Over losing Willow

Creek? Or could she possibly be crying for him? He didn't want to raise his expectations. Brodie knew he was begging for more heartbreak, but he couldn't seem to quell the hope bubbling in his chest. He had to know for sure.

Galvanized, he placed his hand on the knob and wrenched open the door.

Deannie gasped and leaped to her feet, the photo album smacking against the hardwood floor. It fluttered open to a page from the past. Gil Hollis was in the photograph, along with a smiling woman and a small girl on a pony. That red-haired, freckle-faced child had to be Deannie.

She must have unearthed the album from the junk piles stacked high in the bedroom. In that instant Brodie understood her. She'd dreamed her whole life of recapturing what she'd lost fifteen years ago. Years lost to her forever. Years destroyed by his father. Years filled with pain and misery and loneliness. Rafe had been to blame for Deannie's sorrow, and no matter how he might wish it, there was no way Brodie could repair the damage.

Raising a trembling hand, Deannie stared at him. "Brodie," she croaked, a myriad of fearful sensations slapping her hard and fast. "Wh-what are you doing here?"

✺ 16 ✺

"I might ask you the same question." His black eyes narrowed to dark accusing slits, his brows knotted over the bridge of his nose.

Deannie's heart fluttered as helpless as a trapped butterfly beating its wings against a jelly jar.

How handsome he was!

Dressed in his tuxedo, his hair combed off his forehead, his hips cocked forward in that don't-mess-with-me pose, he was the most magnificent man she'd ever seen, and Deannie had been inches from becoming his wife.

"Are you all right?" he murmured.

She nodded, unable to speak for the emotions sticking to the roof of her mouth like peanut butter.

"You didn't twist your ankle or sprain your arm?"

She shook her head.

"You took quite a jump from that second-story window."

"I landed on my feet," she said at last, still captured by his gaze and feeling claustrophobic.

"Why did you leave me, Deannie?" he asked quietly. "Why did you make me stand up there all alone, waiting and waiting for you?"

"I never meant to hurt you," she whimpered.

"Don't lie to me." He walked across the floor until they stood face to face, and Deannie could feel his hot, angry breath on her cheek. "I know who you are, Deanna Renee Hollis."

A gasp echoed in the room. Strange, she didn't think the noise came from her lips, but it must have.

"H-h-how long have you known?" she stuttered.

"Matilda Jennings just informed me."

Her knees wobbled, and Deannie feared they'd buckle beneath her if she remained standing. "I need to sit down."

"I'm sure you do." His tone held no emotion at all.

Placing her hand on the back of the sofa, she eased herself down and took a deep breath. When she'd fled the ranch house, she'd assumed she would never have to face Brodie again.

Now he was here, glaring at her as if she was his worst enemy, and Deannie realized just how badly she'd treated him. She deserved every ounce of his scorn.

"You planned to marry me to get your hands on Willow Creek." He paced the floorboards before her, the ancient wood groaning and creaking beneath his weight.

She couldn't deny it. "Yes. But that was before I knew you."

Brodie gritted his teeth. "You should have told me

the truth. It wouldn't have changed the way I felt about you."

"Wouldn't it? Would you have given me the job as your housekeeper if you'd known I was Gil Hollis's daughter?"

"Maybe. We'll never know, will we?"

"I can't undo what I did, Brodie. I wish I could. I made a mistake. A big mistake. I realized that when I found this letter." She handed him Rafe's letter and the cashier's check for twenty-five thousand dollars.

Brodie read it, then looked up at her with sorrow in his eyes. "I'm not my father, Deannie, and you should know that by now. I'm sorry for what Rafe did to you. It hurts me in innumerable ways, but I can't undo the past either."

"I know that," she said miserably. "That's why I couldn't go through with the wedding. I couldn't make you pay for your father's sins."

Brodie's jaw clenched.

He had every right to hate her. She'd done nothing but lie to him from the start. How she wanted to reach out to him, to touch that dear face, to fall on her knees and beg his forgiveness. But could he forgive her?

Brodie shook his head. "It took so much for me to trust you. I was so afraid to love, so terrified I'd end up like my mother, caring about someone who couldn't love me back." His laugh was an ugly cackle without a trace of mirth. "Despite my best intentions, despite the care I took, I fell right into the same trap."

"It wasn't like that."

"No?"

Miserably, she shook her head.

"What was it like?"

"From the moment I saw you, I knew I was in trouble."

"There's one thing I need to know," he said.

"Yes?" She clasped her hands together in her lap.

"I want the truth." He swung his hard gaze, knife-blade sharp, at her.

Silently, she nodded.

"Do you love me?"

"I love you. With all my heart and soul. That's why I ran from the wedding. I couldn't do it. I couldn't marry you under false pretenses."

"Lord, Deannie, how I'd like to believe you." He looked at her, and his eyes were red-rimmed and close to tears.

"I'm so sorry, Brodie. There's nothing I can do to change what I've done, but I'm begging you to give me a second chance. Please? Could we try again? And this time there'll be no more secrets keeping us from truly getting to know each other."

BRODIE'S GAZE SWEPT HER TREMBLING BODY. He couldn't deny the yearning inside him. He wanted her, no matter her faults. She'd laid everything on the line, confessed her failings. Now it was his turn, for he wasn't without culpability.

All this time, he'd been afraid to give himself completely to her. He'd held his emotions in reserve, ready to pull them back if she showed signs of not living up to his ideal. He'd uselessly been trying to protect himself. If he loved, then he loved.

And he loved Deannie with a timeless yearning.

Urged on by the feelings sweeping through his body, Brodie trod heavily across the floor toward her. Without another word, he gathered her into his arms and planted his fiery brand upon her trembling mouth.

Lord, had anyone ever tasted so sweet? All his suffering disappeared in her embrace. Her arms went around his neck. Her grateful fingers entangled in his hair. Her quiet noises of pleasure stoked his emotions to a fever pitch.

"Look me in the eyes, Deanna Rene Hollis," Brodie said, breaking his lips from hers and cupping her petite chin in his palm.

She gulped but held his gaze.

"Do you want to come home to Willow Creek for good?"

"Not if it means hurting you. I'd rather leave forever than have you doubt my love."

"Shh." He placed one finger over her lips. "Answer my question. Do you want to assume your rightful place as mistress of Willow Creek? Do you want to be my wife and live on this land for the rest of your life? Do you want to have our children here and watch them grow? Do you want to mend the hurt our fathers caused so long ago?"

"Oh, Brodie." Deannie sighed. "I've dreamed of this moment for fifteen years. Coming home. Finding a man to love. A man as good and kind and strong as you. At last that moment has arrived, and all my suffering has ended. You are all I've ever wanted. I do, I do, I do."

EPILOGUE

One year later...

It was the Fourth of July again, and Willow Creek was a hotbed of activity.

Brodie manned the smoker, tongs in hand, chuckling at the sweet bedlam that had overtaken the ranch.

Underneath the canopy, Emma and Kenny followed Phillip who'd started toddling. Kenny was one year sober. He was working for Brodie as ranch foreman and doing a damn fine job. He and Emma had moved into the old log cabin, and they were adding an addition and expanding the place. With Deannie's approval, they divided up the ranch and gave Kenny his half.

In the pool Brodie had put in, Buster and Angel, wearing water wings, splashed around in the shallow end with the other little kids at the holiday bash. Their parents and the older children were playing Marco Polo in the deep end. Their friends had come along with the ranch hands, who had the day off, and their families. There was a ping-pong table set up and horseshoes.

Music played from outdoor speakers. They set colorful umbrellas up poolside, offering respite from the sun. Food was everywhere. Trays of fresh fruits and veggies. Cakes. Cookies. Pies.

Sipping a beer, Cooter Gates stood on the porch step close to where Brodie stood.

"It's been a long time since Willow Creek has been this happy." The elderly man smiled. "I never thought I'd live to see this day."

"To be honest, neither did I." Brodie took the brisket from the smoker and settled it onto a foil-lined tray.

"Is it done?" Deannie, standing on tiptoes, came to peek over his shoulder. "The troops are grumbling for your brisket."

"Yep." Brodie snagged his wife in the crook of his arm. They'd married on May twenty-six, a year to the day after they met. They'd spent the time since their almost-wedding to the real deal getting to know each other inside and out as they healed the pieces of their broken pasts together.

He kissed her, and her cheeks pinked in that sexy blush of hers. Then he kissed her again because he simply couldn't get enough. She still took his breath away, and his heart beat quicker every time he saw her. He would never have guessed it was possible to love someone this much.

Emma came over with Phillip in her arms, a wide grin on her face. "Have you told him yet?"

Deannie blushed again and shook her head.

"Told me what?" Brodie asked, covering the brisket with foil to keep it warm.

Emma looked as if she were bursting to share Deannie's news. "It's not for me to say."

Brodie stared at her. "Is something wrong?"

"No," she said. "At least I don't think so."

Alarm rippled over him as he realized just exactly how much he had at stake. "Deannie? What is it?"

"I wanted to wait until tonight to tell you while we watched the fireworks, but since Emma spilled the beans—"

Yes? He could hardly breathe, terrified that something bad had happened.

But Deannie's wide grin put him completely at ease. "I went to the doctor yesterday—"

His fear was back. "Are you sick? What's happened?"

"I've got a touch of morning sickness, but other than that—"

"M...morning sickness?" As the implication of her words swept over him, total joy filled Brodie's heart. "You're pregnant."

"Yes, we are." Her sweet smile lit him up inside.

A baby. They were having a baby of their own.

"Are you happy?"

"My love," he cried, swinging her into his arms and spinning her around. "I have never been happier!"

"I'm thinking if it's a girl we could name her Melinda."

"After my mother." His throat tightened, and he kissed her again. "And if it's a boy, we'll call him Gil."

"Oh, Brodie." Joyful tears misted her eyes.

In that moment, surrounded by family and friends, Brodie realized all his dreams had come true, and all the losses he and Deannie had suffered had been wiped away. A clean slate. A whole new beginning for Willow Creek Ranch. They'd learned from the mistakes of their past, and they could walk confidently into a bright future together.

And as he kissed his wife again there underneath the brightly colored umbrella, Brodie knew his yearning heart had at long last been filled.

ॐ

DEAR READER,

Readers are an author's life blood and the stories couldn't happen without you. Thank you so much for reading. If you enjoyed *Brodie,* I would so appreciate a review. You have no idea how much it means!

If you'd like to keep up with my latest releases, you can sign up for my newsletter @ https://loriwilde.com/sign-up/.

Please turn the page for an excerpt of the next book in the Texas Rascals series, *Dan.* Click to preorder Dan.

To check out my other books, you can visit me on the web @ www.loriwilde.com.

EXCERPT: DAN

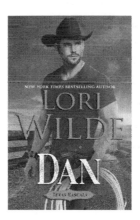

Raleigh Travers needed a job—badly.

She'd dressed carefully for the interview in faded jeans, a navy blue, ribbed tank top and scuffed cowboy boots. Her copper-colored hair hung down her back in a thick, single braid, and she'd tied a red bandanna around her head to keep perspiration from her eyes. She hoped she looked tough, serious and in control.

Turning her battered brown Ford pickup off the main

highway, she rumbled onto a graveled road. She goosed the cranky truck up a steady incline, and a chalky cloud of dust billowed beneath the worn tires. Wind rushed in through the open window, whipping tendrils of hair into her face. Flipping down the visor, she retrieved a pair of aviator sunglasses and pushed them up on her nose.

She drummed fingers on the steering wheel, blew out her breath and leaned over to turn on the radio. Ernest Tubb was singing "Drivin' Nails in My Coffin."

The old tune grated on her jittery nerves. She snapped off the radio and lowered the brim of her cowboy hat. She *had* to get this job. If she couldn't come up with the rent money by Monday, she and Caleb would be out on the street.

"Raleigh, you're gonna have to do some tall talkin'," she said to her reflection in the rearview mirror.

Pa's pitiful insurance settlement was gone. During the previous six months she'd done her best to find work, but she'd been repeatedly turned down for count-less jobs— jobs she was perfectly capable of performing. Even old friends and customers who knew she was a dam good farrier denied her a chance. They all said the same thing—she was too small, too young, too feminine to be doing such rough labor.

Funny, no one had thought that way when she'd worked side by side with her father, shoeing horses from dawn until dusk, but then she'd just been Will Travers's tomboy daughter. Now, while she struggled to get her own business started, the townsfolk refused to take her seriously.

Over and over, she'd been advised to find work

waiting tables or typing reports or watching children. Some even suggested she find a husband. As if this were twentieth century instead of a new millennium.

Marriage? She snorted. With a younger brother to support, dating was the last thing on her mind.

Besides, she couldn't bear the pain of falling in love again. Immediately she thought of Jack and the awful events that had irrevocably altered her life. The familiar ache echoed inside her like lonely whispers in an empty dream.

Raleigh tossed her head. No. She would *not* relive past sorrows. Her future held more pressing concerns than self- pity.

Gritting her teeth, she grasped the steering wheel tighter and thought of her upcoming interview. West of town, a new owner had started renovations on a ramshackle horse ranch. She hoped to find the present management more receptive to a female farrier than the hardheaded, shortsighted citizens of Rascal, Texas.

Up ahead she could see the entrance to the ranch. Barbed wire gave way to white wooden corral fencing. Above the gateway hung a brand-new six-foot sign proclaiming *McClintock Dude Ranch.*

Dude ranch? In Rascal?

Raleigh smiled and hoped the newcomer's wallet matched his flair for farfetched fantasies. The cost of making this project work would not come cheap.

Bumping over the cattle guard, Raleigh lumbered onto the barren landscape of sagebrush, cactus, bull nettles, scrub oaks and yucca. Aiming her pickup down the narrow, rutted road, she rattled and jolted across the arid pasture, and pulled to a stop in the middle of a wide circular driveway.

The place was in the midst of reconstruction. Cement forms were tossed in haphazard heaps beside piles of mounded earth. Stacks of raw lumber decorated the rough terrain, and the smell of fresh paint lingered on the sultry breeze.

A buzzard flew overhead, casting a dark shadow across the pickup's hood. A quiver of fear shivered through her and she had no idea why.

Straight in front of her hulked a large, two-story farmhouse. A bright red barn graced the hill behind the house. Next to the barn sat two stables, a small log cabin, probably meant for the ranch hands, an exercise yard and three separate corrals. Opposite the house sprawled a dilapidated swimming pool, deserted tennis courts, and a faded shuffleboard slab.

The old place was a getting a fresh start. Who was behind it?

Her pulse danced. Raleigh hankered for a fresh start too.

A mix of Thoroughbreds and quarter horses grazed in the fields. Two dozen at least. Enough to net her well over two thousand dollars if she got the job of shoeing them all.

She opened the pickup door and swung to the ground. Her bootheels sunk into the yielding sand. Tucking her fingertips into her back pockets, she scanned the area.

No one in sight.

Ignore the sweaty palms. You're calm. You're cool. You've got this. Braid bouncing between her shoulder blades, she stalked across the exercise yard. Called out, "Anybody home?"

No answer.

She climbed over the corral gate and stopped to scratch the nose of a friendly gelding Thoroughbred who wandered over. "Hey, boy," she cooed.

The horse nuzzled her arm in greeting.

"Where's your owner?" Curious, she stooped over, lifted the Thoroughbred's right foreleg and examined his shoe. He definitely needed a new set.

She clicked her tongue, pulled a sugar cube from her pocket and offered it to the gelding.

"Hey, you! You there! What do you think you're doing?" A rough masculine voice said.

Raleigh's head snapped up.

The horse nickered. She dropped the gelding's leg, turned. Her sunglasses slipped down on her nose. She pushed them back up, and squinted at the tall, commanding figure striding toward her.

Thick eyebrows formed a frowning V on his wide forehead. A stubble of heavy beard enhanced his angular jaw. He wore tight jeans and a blue chambray work shirt with the sleeves rolled up, revealing hairy, muscular forearms. A black cowboy hat rode his head. He towered over her, obstructing her view of the sky. Broad of chest and trim of waist, he presented an appealing if somewhat threatening package.

"You talking to me?" She pointed a hand at herself. An odd stab of excitement raced through her. They exchanged a searing glance.

"I don't see anyone else messing around with my

horse, so I must be talking to you. Who are you?" he demanded.

Not one to be intimidated, even by a man twice her size, Raleigh drew herself up to her full five foot nothing and knotted her hands into fists.

"I'm Raleigh Travers. Who are you?"

The man took a determined step toward her.

Raleigh stood her ground.

He reached over and clamped a large paw on her shoulder.

Whoa there you handsy buzzard. Reflexively, Raleigh turned and drove her arm backward, jabbing her elbow straight into his lean, hard, abs.

The instant she let loose, it hit her who he was— she'd just assaulted her potential boss!

Preorder Dan Now.

ALSO BY LORI WILDE

TEXAS RASCALS SERIES

ABOUT THE AUTHOR

Lori Wilde is the New York Times, USA Today and Publishers' Weekly bestselling author of 87 works of romantic fiction. She's a three time Romance Writers' of America RITA finalist and has four times been nominated for Romantic Times Readers' Choice Award. She has won numerous other awards as well.

Her books have been translated into 26 languages, with more than four million copies of her books sold worldwide.

Her breakout novel, *The First Love Cookie Club*, has been optioned for a TV movie.

Lori is a registered nurse with a BSN from Texas Christian University. She holds a certificate in forensics, and is also a certified yoga instructor.

A fifth generation Texan, Lori lives with her husband, Bill, in the Cutting Horse Capital of the World; where they run Epiphany Orchards, a writing/creativity retreat for the care and enrichment of the artistic soul.

 f 𝕏 ⊙ ⓟ